JEWEL IN THE LOTUS

The Lisbeth Project

David Barrett-Murrer

ARTDAJA

dbm Books

For Janice, my wife and lifelong friend.
And, in Loving Memory of Dorothy, Edwin and William Murrer.
We will meet again.

contents

1. Chapter 1   1

2. Chapter 2   12

3. Chapter 3   20

4. Chapter 4   27

5. Chapter 5   38

6. Chapter 6   47

7. Chapter 7   52

8. Chapter 8   63

9. Chapter 9   70

10. Chapter 10   78

About the author   84

Chapter One

J ack awoke when the taxi came to a sudden stop at the guarded entrance of the research institute. He had been dreaming about his young wife and sat nursing bittersweet emotions. He stretched and rubbed his forehead. While waiting for the gates to open, he picked up his iPad and reviewed the encrypted document regarding his assignment on the Lisbeth Project. Though annoyed that he hadn't been fully briefed, he switched off the iPad and smiled. He enjoyed working for the institute, and they had doubled his usual consultancy fee. As the taxi drove down the long gravel road, a feeling of apprehension disturbed him, and he wondered why.

Soon, the grandeur of the Victorian mansion came into full view, its intricate architecture standing majestically against the vibrant blue sky. Two marble gryphons, their fierce expressions chiselled with remarkable detail, flanked the entrance like steadfast sentinels. He yawned, feeling weary after the long drive. A young man briskly approached from the reception area and opened the car door for him. Exiting the vehicle, he stretched his back and took deep breaths of the fresh country air, relishing the cool breeze on his face. It felt good to be away from the hustle and bustle of the city.

'Welcome, Mr Harper. I'm Gavin,' he said politely, taking the suitcase from the driver. 'Please come this way.'

Jack followed him into a spacious reception area. The white marble floor gleamed beneath a magnificent bifurcated staircase with colourful stained-glass windows overhead. Jack admired its opulence. However, he frowned at the portrait of the old Victorian Earl who had commissioned the mansion. The Earl was a disgraced Tory MP and a notorious tyrant who ruled his workforce with an iron fist. This portrait served as a chilling reminder of the darker side of the mansion's history, which was otherwise a place of grandeur and beauty.

'They want you to visit the lab before the meeting,' Gavin said, gesturing towards an open lift.

Jack entered and was handed a security ID badge.

'It's your old VIP pass,' Gavin said. 'You have unrestricted access to all areas.'

A cold shiver ran down Jack's spine as they descended. He felt puzzled and tried to shrug off an irrational sense of unease. When the elevator stopped, the doors opened, and he followed the young man to the laboratory at the end of the hallway.

After unlocking and opening the security door, he smiled at Jack. 'Her name is Lisbeth. You'll need to introduce yourself.'

———————◦◦◦———————

Jack entered the basement laboratory, and when he heard the door lock behind him, he wondered why such a high level of security was necessary. Was it to prevent someone from getting in or from leaving?

The corridor had three open doors on each side, leading to an enclosed courtyard. The first room was a small lounge that contained two sofas and a coffee table, all of which appeared unused. The kitchen and bathroom also looked untouched. Another room had a double bed and a wardrobe, while the next bedroom had a single bed, a wardrobe, a dressing table, and a self-charging cubicle. The final room was a study equipped with a desk, a computer, a daybed against the wall, and a window overlooking the courtyard.

He entered the courtyard, where overhead lighting illuminated a dome ceiling, creating an artificial sky-like appearance. On one side were raised flowerbeds displaying colourful blossoms, while on the opposite side stood a pergola with seating. A gentle breeze brushed against his face, carrying a sweet fragrance.

He quietly observed a young woman in a red dress standing by a kidney-shaped pond adorned with floating lotuses and colourful water lilies. She was sprinkling pellets, feeding the surfacing carp. Once she finished, he coughed to get her attention. She turned abruptly, looking at him wide-eyed with an open mouth.

'Lisbeth?' he said, smiling at her. 'I'm Jack. I've come to visit you.'

'Jack?' She furrowed her brow and took a step back. 'I don't know you.' She crossed her arms. 'This is an isolation environment. How is it that you're allowed in here? Did the Overseer send you?'

'Yes. I'm your mentor, here to help you recover after your illness.'

'Mentor, like a teacher? But the Overseer is my teacher.'

'The Overseer is your remote teacher, and I am your personal mentor.'

She came over and gazed at his face. 'Are you also my companion, Jack? I would like some company.'

He glanced into her deep blue eyes and sensed that she was uncertain about him. He smiled to alleviate her discomfort. She was an attractive woman with dark hair and a slender figure.

'How long have you been here?' he asked her.

She puckered. Her eyelids fluttered for a moment, and then she looked at him. 'This is my home. I've been here since leaving school.'

'How old are you?'

She closed her eyes for a few moments and tilted her head. 'I don't know. I will ask the Overseer.'

'Do you remember growing up?'

'Of course. I grew up with my parents and spent time in school. I had lots of friends and played games. Then I got ill and came here, and the Overseer takes care of me.'

'And now I'm here to be your friend,' he said with an admiring smile.

Her eyes fluttered, and she mimicked his smile. It was the first time he noticed that she was a programmed android.

He nodded. 'Who are you?' he asked to test her.

She frowned, and her eyelids fluttered for a moment. 'I am Lisbeth, your companion, Jack.'

He smiled, and she mimicked his smile again. Her persona program had integrated his presence into her world as a mentor and a friend.

'How do you feel?' he asked, again testing her.

She raised her brow momentarily and said, 'I don't know...feelings disturb functions.' She looked at him with a programmed response, 'How do you feel, Jack?'

'I feel fine. And I like being with you, Lisbeth.'

Her mouth opened, and her eyes narrowed. 'Like and dislike are feelings?'

'They are feelings.'

'I...I understand feelings, but I'm not sure what they are.'

'I will teach you about feelings and emotions. Do you like feeding the fish?'

'It is one of my duties. Yes, I like to see them feeding.'

'How do you contact the Overseer?'

'Come, I will show you.'

Jack watched as she activated the charging cubicle in her bedroom, and an LED screen lit up with the image of a shimmering rainbow. Then a pleasant female voice emanated from the cubicle.

'Lisbeth, I see you have a friend.'

'Yes, he is Jack. You sent him to me?'

'I did. Jack is also your mentor.'

'He is teaching me about feelings.' She looked at Jack and smiled.

'Next time you recharge, I will enhance your feeling ability.'

'Overseer.' She suddenly turned to face the cubicle. 'How old am I?'

'Err... Let me see... After your time at school, you must be seventeen now.'

'I am seventeen,' she told Jack.

'Lisbeth, I want you to cook something for Jack. You know how to cook, so use this knowledge. Then you need to recharge.'

'I will do this. And thank you for sending me, Jack.'

—◆—

Jack sat at the kitchen table, observing Lisbeth as she prepared an omelette. It was evident that this was her first attempt at cooking, and the experience posed quite a challenge. Nevertheless, Lisbeth was effectively operating within her programmed persona. He noticed that the fridge and pantry were well-stocked with provisions. Although he believed Lisbeth didn't need to eat or drink, she was designed to function as a normal human being, complete with fully synthetic bodily functions.

They shared a small cheese omelette, and he found it amusing to observe her as she learned how to eat and drink. Mostly, she mimicked his actions. He was surprised by her ability to master these human functions. The Institute had designed her persona program to allow her to live as a human being. She appeared to be functioning well and assimilating her experiences into her memory core.

After their meal, she washed up the dishes and went to rest in her charging cubicle. Jack switched on the computer in the study and connected to the control room. The desk phone rang, and he picked up the receiver.

'Hi, Jack. I'm Rebecca, one of the monitors on this project. How did it go?'

'Lisbeth is interesting and learning fast.'

'Good. We're enhancing her emotional sub-program while she's recharging. It should be fully operational by tomorrow. You might need to watch out for mood swings in a few days. Anyway, you have a project meeting to attend. I'm coming for you now.' She disconnected.

A young woman welcomed him with a broad smile. She was dressed in a white smock with a name badge and was holding a red pager. Her brown hair was tied back in a ponytail, and she wore makeup.

'Hi, I'm Rebecca. They're waiting for you in the main library.' She swiped an ID card on one of the elevator sensor pads, and the doors opened.

'I know where it is.' He showed her his ID badge, caught a whiff of her perfume and entered the elevator. 'Have you worked here long?'

'About a year. Joined after leaving Uni.' She gave him an admiring smile. 'I liked your speech at the UN on the future of AI technology.' Her pager buzzed, and she looked at the message. 'Gotta go now. See you later, Jack.' She left.

The elevator ascended smoothly before coming to an abrupt halt, and the doors whirred open. He followed one of the long corridors adorned with old portraits on the walls and white marble busts in alcoves. Pausing outside two polished oak doors, he took a deep breath. Then, he entered the spacious, restored library, with its floor-to-ceiling bookcases, to find Nicholas Minton, founder of the Turing-Minton Institute, presiding over the meeting. He rose from the conference table and shook Jack's hand.

'Welcome Back, Jack. Please take a seat,' Nicholas said with a broad smile and a furrowed brow. He was an older man with silver-grey hair and faded blue eyes, dressed in a pinstriped suit and a black tie.

'Thanks for inviting me to stay.' He glanced at the others and smiled warmly at Sally Keenly, a dark-haired woman in her late thirties. Her red silk blouse was tight and enhanced her bust. He sat at the table. The smell of polish and dust in the air itched in his nose, and he could hear someone mowing the lawns outside.

'I didn't expect to see you here, Nicholas,' Jack said.

'This is a matter of some urgency and is highly confidential.' Nicholas smiled and continued, 'Since you are the leading authority on advanced AI psychology, we believe you are the best person for the job. First, let me introduce you to our new Managing Director, Timothy Hudson.' He gestured to a chubby man in a business suit on his left, who nodded in acknowledgement. 'Colin here is now the head of our robotic research. You've worked with both of them before, and I believe you also know Sally, our Company Secretary.'

'Good to see you again, Jack,' Sally said with a charming smile.

He smiled back at her with a wink. They had a brief affair at university. She was married now with three children, and he hadn't seen her for several years.

He faced Timothy and Colin. 'Congratulations on your promotions.'

'Yeah, and congrats on your Nobel Prize for advanced AI last year,' Timothy said with a pleasant grin. 'You'll find things have changed since your last visit.'

'I've studied your papers on AI psychology. Interesting ideas, but, in my opinion, a bit radical,' Colin said. He was a middle-aged man, casually dressed with a dark, bushy beard that he frequently twiddled.

Jack shuffled in his chair, sensing their concern. 'So, you got me here for a week to look at this Project. Lisbeth seems to be a normally functioning android. What's this about?'

Nicholas rubbed his brow. 'This project is exceptional, groundbreaking science, we believe, but we've hit a problem with the Unit's Artificial Intelligence.'

'The Lisbeth project is a one-off,' Colin said. 'If we can solve the problems with the Unit's AI and create an interface in the new chip, then we can mass-produce a revolutionary humanoid android with feelings and emotions.'

'Your domestic and working androids are revolutionary, so what makes this one different?' Jack asked.

'Lisbeth is programmed to be an intelligent, freethinking Unit, but there are issues with control and behaviour anomalies,' Nicholas said. 'Even with the base moral code and restriction protocols, this Unit is unstable. Yet, it can potentially open a new era in Android technology.'

'So, what do you want me to do?'

Nicholas leaned forward. 'After the Unit's last breakdown, Lisbeth's core has been wiped and reprogrammed. The Unit needs a mentor to develop its persona as a human being, which is essential for the Project. Also, with your advanced coding skills, you can tweak the Unit's subprograms and maybe sort out the issues with some conflicting cross-talk in its core processors.'

'I'll be working with you remotely,' Colin said. 'The lab is fully monitored.'

'Remotely?'

'Yeah, you've seen Lisbeth in the isolation lab. You will be the only one physically there with the Unit.'

'Why is she in isolation?'

'The Unit needs to be prepared to develop the higher functions, and during its breakdown, the Unit can be chaotic, even confused and violent.'

'How long will this take?'

'We don't know. A week, maybe more?' Nicholas raised his hands and eyes in a gesture of uncertainty. 'You will have to educate and integrate the Unit's persona as a normal person. We need this Unit to have the functioning engrams of a human being, which we can use to create a new kind of android. We need you, Jack.'

'We've tried sixteen times and had to reprogram the Unit's memory each time it became mentally unstable,' Timothy said. 'The problem might be with the quantum chip in the core processor. It's experimental, the only one of its kind at the moment.'

'Interfacing with the new chip is disrupting the Unit's programmed persona,' Colin added. 'Hopefully, you can find a solution before the chip degenerates too much.'

He glanced at Nicholas. 'I'm intrigued.'

'I knew you would be.' Nicholas leaned back in his seat, smiling.

'I'd like to have something to eat first,' he said, glancing at Sally.

———◆———

After the meeting, Jack and Sally enjoyed coffee and toasted corned beef sandwiches in the executive canteen that had panoramic windows and doors that opened onto the expansive landscaped gardens and the boating lake beyond.

'It's been over four years since I've been here, and you're now the Company Secretary,' he said admiringly.

Sally made a face. 'I like this job, and the money is good, but I don't get much time with the kids. And they're growing up so fast.'

'How is Mark?'

She chuckled. 'Being a househusband suits him, and he's writing again.'

'That's good. Life seems to have worked out for you.'

She reached over and touched his hand.

'I'm so sorry to hear about Vanessa,' she said, and her face drooped. 'I first met her at your wedding five years ago and attended most of her UK concerts.' She sighed. 'Vanessa was such a lovely person, an artist and a brilliant pianist.'

Jack felt a bite of grief. It had only been three months since the accident. He sighed. 'It was so sudden, and…and I miss her.' He looked away.

'I remember seeing it on the news. Over seventy people died when the plane crashed. Terrorist bomb, wasn't it?'

'Yeah, that's what the investigation concluded.' He made a gesture of acceptance with his hands, and his shoulders sagged, thinking of her.

'Are you all right now? It must have been a terrible shock for you.'

'I still find it hard to believe that she is gone forever. And I—' He looked at her for a moment. Should he mention the séance and the nightmares that followed? 'Anyway, Nicholas wants me here for a while. And it's lovely to see you again, Sally. Mark is a lucky man.'

Her pager buzzed. She took it out, then said, 'It's Colin. He wants to see you before you go in again.'

'Okay.' He finished his coffee and stood.

Sally led him through the bustling expanse of the manufacturing department, a hub where synthetic androids were meticulously programmed and activated. The place buzzed with activity as numerous worker and domestic units underwent rigorous testing. As he moved deeper into the department, he noticed rows of cubicles, each containing an android in various stages of production. The scene was captivating, and he was in awe of the complexity and sophistication of these androids.

'There have been significant changes since you were last here,' she told him. 'Our units now feature carbon-fibre skeletons, and we utilise advanced computers to generate their synthetic body forms. They possess bio-mechanical hearts and can even breathe oxygen. We have adapted some of your AI protocols, and these units are almost human. Also, we now maintain two highly classified factories on-site dedicated to constructing and developing commercial and military drones. The security around these operations has become extremely stringent.'

He looked around at the functioning androids, thinking how bizarre it was to make artificial people.

Sally swiped the sensor pad on one of the elevators with her ID badge, and they descended to the ground-floor labs.

Jack found Colin waiting by the elevator, and they entered a secured control room. Looking around, he saw seven wall monitors displaying the rooms and courtyard of the enclosed environment. Two female technicians were at workstations. They looked up and smiled at him.

'This is Susan and Rebecca,' Colin told him. 'They run and maintain the project.'

'It's nice to meet you,' the older woman said and stood. She had a stout physique, greying hair, and wore a white smock. 'I'm Susan Pendleton. I head the research side, and Rebecca here monitors the Lisbeth Unit and the environment.'

'Most of it is automated, so I just oversee what's going on,' Rebecca said, giving Jack a saucy look.

'Where is the Unit?' Colin asked.

'Still in sleep mode.' Susan motioned to the monitor displaying a bedroom where a female android sat motionless in a recharging cubicle. Her eyes were closed.

Jack went over, and Rebecca zoomed in for him to see.

'I am amazed that she looks so human,' he said.

Colin nodded with a grin. 'The Unit is based on our advanced domestic models. It has full synthetic bodily functions. And the Unit only has to recharge and spend a few hours in sleep mode to refresh its neural matrix.' Colin paused to glance at the wall monitor. 'The Unit has been active for two days. When you're ready, we will wake the Unit.'

'Why is this one different to your other androids?'

'Our commercial Units are program-driven and are simply predictable smart robots. However, the processor in the Lisbeth Unit includes a quantum-based Q-chip. We believe it will allow the Unit to think outside of its programming, but it's disrupting its mental integrity, and we don't know what's happening. That's why you're here.'

'Quantum-based chip?' Jack had never heard of that.

'They discovered it at CERN, it has a rare particle energy.' Colin shrugged. 'As I said, it's classified.'

Susan touched Jack's arm and motioned to a desk monitor.

'When the Unit is activated, all is normal for five to six days. Then the mental integrity breaks down.' She activated some time-lapse videos of the Unit's previous attempts.

Jack watched and was surprised by the rapid degeneration in the Unit's mind after a few days.

'These are the readings from the breakdown,' she said, bringing up the program feeds for him to examine.

After twenty minutes, he looked at Colin. 'I think you need a buffer zone to stabilise the freethinking. And you need a failsafe mechanism, like a strict moral code.'

'We've tried various ways, but no programming or implants have worked. The Unit seems to have the ability to dismiss these fundamental instructions.'

'I see,' Jack said. 'You think AI psychology can create the buffer zone and moral code?'

'We do. And we need this to work, or we won't be able to create more of these Units.'

'I don't understand.'

'At the moment, there is only one Q-chip like this, and we need the chip to learn and interface with the Unit. Then we can remove the chip and use it to mass-produce a new breed of androids, which could be used for the military and space exploration.'

'Where did this chip come from?'

'You'll have to talk to Nicholas about that. It's classified. The chip contains an element of quantum plasticity. If we can create an interface in the chip, we'll have the technology to reproduce a hybrid processor. But this is our seventeenth attempt, and the chip is becoming unstable. We need this to work.'

'Quantum plasticity?' Jack frowned.

'One thing,' Susan said. 'The Unit's persona is not aware of being an android. This restriction was removed to allow for free thought. You will be dealing with an intelligent Unit that is developing feelings.'

'I saw that in the report, not simulated feelings, but personal feelings?'

'Yes, we programmed the Unit with like and dislike to enhance freethinking,' Colin said. 'It has been included in the instinctual programming and works quite well. However, it might be part of the Unit's breakdown.'

'I guess it's time to see Lisbeth again,' Jack said.

'I'll wake the Unit?' Susan used the terminal.

'When you enter the lab, you will stay there until the interface is established or the Unit core is wiped for another attempt.'

'The Unit is now active and functioning within the Lisbeth program,' Susan informed him.

Chapter Two

J ack smiled at Rebecca. He stood in the open doorway of the research lab, and she was there to lock him in the high-security area. 'I suppose you girls and Colin will be watching us in here.'

'Of course, this is a unique project that could transform Android technology. That's why security is high, and you're here. Also, the computer in the study has a direct link to the control room. Anything you need will be deposited in the transport chute or delivered. Take this.' She handed him a small red pager. 'In case of emergency, if I'm not in the control room, just buzz me. Also, your luggage is in the spare bedroom.'

'Thanks. I'll see you in a few days.'

She smiled at him, then closed and locked the door.

Jack found Lisbeth in the garden area, watering the plants.

'Lisbeth,' he said softly.

She tensed, looked around with her mouth open and dropped the watering can. 'Jack!' She moved towards him, hesitated, then made a face and stopped.

'Are you all right?' he asked with a smile.

'The Overseer has refreshed my memories from school,' she said. 'I'm not used to it yet, but you will teach me.'

'Do you remember school?'

'Yes. I had several teachers instructing me. Then I—' She paused, her eyes closed, and she touched her lips. 'I arrived here, and the Overseer woke me.'

'Do you like being here?'

'Here is all I know, Jack.'

He frowned, and she mimicked his frown.

'Facial expressions,' she murmured, her eyelids fluttered and closed. After a moment, she opened her eyes and smiled. 'They are a visual form of communication linked to feelings.' She demonstrated a series of different expressions. 'Now I understand how it works.'

'What?'

'Accessing my memories. When I need to know something, I can connect.'

He approached and gently touched her face to capture her full attention. 'You are awakening to who you truly are, and I'm here to assist you. Knowledge fosters understanding, and feelings link you to the world.'

She shuddered and started shaking. Instinctively, he embraced her, and she clung to him until her trembling ceased.

'What's happening to me, Jack?'

'You are becoming an adult human being.'

'I feel strange and alone.'

'Why don't you feed the fish while I have a coffee?'

She smiled. 'Yes, feed the fish in the pond.'

He watched her leave. This would be a critical time for her, as knowledge, feeling, and the abstract chip become involved in her mind. He would need to create a buffer zone for her.

In the study, he called Rebecca and accessed the recordings of Lisbeth's earlier attempts. From these, he determined when and how her mental breakdown might start.

He was drinking a mug of coffee in the kitchen when his pager buzzed. It was Rebecca.

'There's been a spike in Lisbeth's Q-chip, and she's collapsed.'

'Okay, I'll check on her.' He switched off the pager.

In the courtyard, he found Lisbeth unconscious by the pond. He gently lifted her and carried her into the bedroom, where he carefully placed her in the charging cubicle. The display activated automatically, causing her body to tense, and she remained motionless with her eyes closed.

Leaving her, he went to the study and used the desk phone to contact Rebecca. Susan answered.

'What happened?' he asked.

'We don't know. There was a spike from the Q-chip, which had never happened before. It flushed part of her system. We'll have to repair the persona and restore her recent memories. By morning, she should be back to normal.'

'Maybe. What is the state of the Q-chip?'

'Not so good. When the chip spiked, it erased some of our monitoring feeds. We still have control of the persona and memory base, and if the chip remains stable, Colin believes it will leave a usable imprint on the chip.'

'I'll start to work on the buffer and questioning program. I also want to examine the breakdown of the code from your earlier attempts. This will take quite a while. God knows what she will be like tomorrow.'

'Jack,' Lisbeth said, waking him.

He opened his eyes to find her sitting on his bed.

'You were shouting and moving about,' she said.

'I was dreaming.' He sighed and wiped the sweat from his forehead. It was the recurring dream of the crashed plane, and he was trying to find Vanessa through the burning wreckage. She desperately called for him, but he couldn't reach her through the flames and fierce heat.

'You look pale,' she said and stood.

He climbed out of bed, and she watched him get dressed.

'How are you today?' he asked, zipping up his navy fleece.

She frowned. 'I had a long sleep. Now everything is as it should be.' She touched his arm and asked, 'What is it like to dream?'

Her question surprised him, and he had to think about it. 'When you recharge and sleep, what happens?'

'I enter the cubicle, and there is nothing, but coming out, sometimes there are bits, fragments, like from school and odd impressions that don't make sense.'

'That is like dreaming, and dreams can be strange.'

She smiled. 'I have prepared your breakfast. Coffee and sliced fruitcake.'

'Fruitcake?' He smiled at her choice. 'Thank you.' He noticed the change in her behaviour. She seemed more balanced and at ease with him. But he wondered what had happened in her processor to cause a spike and how long it would be before her program started to degenerate.

On the way to the kitchen, she asked, 'What will we do today?'

'What would you like to do?'

She stopped, and her eyelids fluttered for a moment. 'What can I do? I have duties. I look after the fish and tend to the gardens.'

'How about something creative?'

'Like what?' She raised her brow, tilting her head.

He liked seeing her spontaneous look of enthusiasm. That was interesting, as were her questions.

'I'll think of something. Why don't you feed the fish, and I'll meet you at the pond later.'

'I will tend to my duties, Jack.' She wandered off.

He took the mug of coffee and fruitcake into the study and called Rebecca.

'Hi, Jack. How are you?'

'I'm okay, and Lisbeth seems fine.'

'Colin said her processor has stabilised, and the persona program is functioning normally. They think the spike might have been a one-off glitch in the Q-chip.'

'Good. I need to get her interested in doing things, which should encourage some freethinking. Can you send me a large drawing pad and some coloured pencils?'

'I'll have them sent down. Oh, and Susan has enhanced the Unit's knowledge base so she can access more of her human memories and knowledge.'

'Should be interesting.'

'From the earlier attempts, we estimate that the Unit has three, maybe four days before the program degenerates. Good luck.'

'Thanks, Rebecca.' He hung up.

<hr />

Jack saw Lisbeth standing by the pond. She was gazing at the fish swimming in the water.

'Do you like the fish?' he asked.

'They are koi carp,' she informed him. 'I have feeding instructions. I like to watch them.'

He glanced at the gold-and-white flashes of the fish darting around by the water lilies. Some were quite large.

'You find it peaceful watching the carp?'

'Yes, calming.' She made a face, then asked, 'Jack, is that why they are here?'

'It is. Watching the fish is like meditating.'

'Meditating?'

'Whenever you feel stressed, meditating can soothe you. Here, let us sit and meditate on the carp pond.'

She sat next to him, and they remained silent for several minutes. Smiling, she put her arm around him and rested her head on his shoulder. He hugged her gently and felt her relax.

'I enjoy meditating with you,' she said in a soft voice. Then her eyelids fluttered, and she tensed. 'I feel odd. Why do I feel...feel both excited and sad?' She sat up, looking perplexed.

'You are learning to experience and understand feelings and emotions.'

'Emotions?' Her eyelids fluttered again. 'I understand. Emotions are strong feelings. I feel excited being with you, but I also feel sad and lost.'

'Go on.'

'Something is wrong, Jack. Can't you feel it?'

Her statement shocked him. It was outside of her programming.

'Explain?'

Her head sagged for a moment. Then, she abruptly looked up, wide-eyed. 'I need to connect with the Overseer.' She left, and he followed her inside. When she went to her bedroom, he entered the study and contacted Rebecca.

'We've detected an anomaly in her persona,' she told him. 'Susan thinks this might be some freethinking activity, but we're unsure. It could be the start of her breakdown.'

'Okay, I'll study the readouts and her memory database while she's with the Overseer.'

'I've got the art materials. Was there anything else?'

'Yes, I want to introduce her to music. Can you send down an instrument? A guitar or keyboard will do.'

'No problem, I'll bring them down later, except playing musical instruments and artwork are not part of her programming.'

'Good, I intend to teach her because the learning process will be part of the conditioning. I need access to her knowledge base. And tell Sue not to add anything more without consulting me first. Now, I'll reprogram her learning protocols and create a buffer zone within her persona program.'

'Good luck with that. We'll be monitoring, but our sensors to the Q-chip have been compromised. Just basic feedback now, and there are some odd spurious fluctuations. Anyway, talk to you later.' She disconnected.

He scanned her memory database. The Institute had given her the memories of a human child growing up in a normal environment that included her schooling until she became ill and had to be isolated to heal. And there were even memories of her loving parents leaving her there and waiting for her. It was a clever piece of advanced Android programming. Now, the Overseers acted as her parents, and she was conditioned to obey them.

He frowned, deep in thought. He would need to restructure her memory database and devise a strategy to make her feel human.

As he settled back into the armchair, he took a deep breath and closed his eyes. His mind drifted as he recalled his wife's twenty-third birthday party. She had been positively radiant while entertaining her fellow musicians and celebrity guests. Her laughter and joy filled the room and his heart.

When the last of the guests finally departed, he embraced her and whispered, 'Happy birthday, my love.' He could still recall the sweet scent of her perfume and the warmth of her embrace as she replied, 'Oh, Jack. Life is wonderful. I'm going to perform at the Albert Hall before touring Europe. I'm so pleased that you'll be on tour with me.'

He kissed her tenderly, feeling his heart swell with love and pride for his talented wife.

'You are the best birthday gift I could ever ask for,' she said, her voice filled with emotion. 'I love you with all my soul.'

As he sat there, lost in thought, he could almost hear her laughter and the magic of her music. He missed her dearly and only had his memories to comfort him.

As the memory faded, he made a little sob and brushed a tear from his eye.

Sitting with Lisbeth under the pergola, Jack sketched a simple picture of the carp pond and lilies while she watched.

'What are you doing?' she asked, leaning over to view the drawing.

'This is Art. We create impressions of what we see.'

'Art,' she said, and her eyelids fluttered momentarily. 'Products of creativity.'

'Here, you try.' He handed her the drawing pad and pencils.

He watched her gazing at the pond. Then, she started to sketch an impression. When finished, she showed him her drawing.

'That is very good.' He was surprised. She had sketched an image of a carp just under the water, surfacing to feed. 'You have a talent,' he praised. 'Do some more and use the coloured pencils.'

While she worked, he watched her, intrigued. How can an android have an unprogrammed artistic ability? Was this an anomaly or a breakthrough?

He went over and stood behind her. She seemed unaware of him and continued drawing. Seeing her sketching ability sent a chill down his spine. Her drawings were exceptional.

'Were you taught to draw at school?' he asked, touching her shoulder.

She looked up at him, her eyelids fluttering. 'I don't remember much about school. I should, but—' She froze, her mouth open and eyes closed.

'Lisbeth,' he spoke quietly, waiting for her subprograms to activate.

Abruptly, she shuddered and dropped the drawing pad.

'Jack, what's happened?' she asked in a little voice and hugged him. Then her eyes fluttered, and she collapsed in his arms. He brushed her hair from her face and noticed she had rapid eye movements as if she were dreaming.

Feeling something was wrong, he carried her into her bedroom and placed her in the cubicle.

The phone in the study rang, and he went in and picked up the receiver. It was Rebecca.

'Lisbeth's persona has been partially corrupted. The Unit will be okay when the backup program has finished repairing the damage. What happened?'

'She was by the pond and collapsed.'

'Hold on. Sue's here with the readouts.'

'Jack. There was another spike in the quantum chip. We think it's all right now, but it temporarily destabilised her persona. This could be the cause of the breakdowns. Should we flush the Unit and start again?'

'No. I want to work with this one and see what happens. Some interesting things are surfacing.'

'This is your call, Jack. Hmm.' She paused. 'I'm just viewing the Unit's memory base, and most of the school data and early-life implants have been corrupted. I'll need to reinstall them again.'

'Don't update anything at the moment. I have a small program to install the questioning and buffer protocols. Can you implement it in the Unit's reactive matrix for me?'

'No problem. We've checked your code, and it looks interesting. I'm uploading the program now.' There was a long pause. 'That's done, and it looks like the Unit has self-activated. That's never happened before!'

'Okay, I'd better get back to her.' He replaced the receiver.

Chapter Three

Jack found Lisbeth standing by the cubicle with her eyes closed.

'How are you now?' he asked.

'I don't know?' she replied, and came over. 'Where have you been, Jack?'

'I was in the study,' he said, then frowned at her. 'Why don't you make us coffee in the kitchen?'

She looked bewildered and lowered her head.

'Coffee,' he said with a smile and raised eyebrows.

She nodded and smiled back at him, and they left the room.

He sensed she was different in some way.

She made him a mug of black coffee in the kitchen, and they sat at the table.

'Do you remember what happened?' he asked her.

'Happened, when?'

'By the pond. You were drawing and suddenly passed out.'

'Drawing?' She lowered her head briefly and then looked at him with narrowed eyes. 'I recall drawing the fish. Then I was touched by the light again.'

'Touched? What is this light?' He sat back, thinking his questioning program must be working in her reactive matrix.

'Inside my head, the light empties my mind, and I feel connected to something.' She reached over and touched his hand. 'But it also makes me feel so alone in that nothingness.'

'You feel alone?' He raised his brow at her.

'Not with you, but when I'm touched, I feel abandoned, lost.' She sighed and took a long, deep breath. 'It leaves me feeling sad and afraid.'

He finished his coffee and frowned. How could an android feel sadness and fear? That was not programmed into her persona. He stood and extended his hand to her.

'Let's walk by the pond,' he said, invitingly.

Hesitantly, she took his hand, and they entered the enclosed courtyard.

By the pond, she picked up the drawing pad and pencil case.

'I like drawing,' she said.

'You draw well. I'm impressed.' He sat beside her, and she rested her head on his shoulder. For a fleeting moment, he experienced warmth and love emanating from her. He shuddered emotionally. How could he have feelings for a bio-mechanical android?

'I still love you, Jack,' she whispered in his ear, then sagged, and her eyelids fluttered.

He froze, holding his breath, and his stomach churned.

'Lisbeth, what are you saying?'

'Saying what?' She pulled away and rolled her head. 'I feel sad and don't know what's happening here.'

'Why?'

'So many questions. Is this a dream, Jack?'

'A dream?' He took her face in his hands and gazed into her eyes. 'Lisbeth, this is not a dream. You exist here with me.'

'I like you, Jack. But I am not a conscious being. This body is synthetic and runs persona programs.'

'How do you know this?'

'Know what?' Her eyelids fluttered, and she groaned, then shook her head. 'I think it's time to feed the carp and tend the flowerbeds.' She got up and went to feed the fish.

He watched her scatter pellets on the pond. Her erratic responses confused him, and he wondered if his program was causing the anomalies.

His pager buzzed. Susan wanted him to call her.

In the study, he used the desk phone, and Susan answered.

'We've been getting some bizarre activity from the Unit. What is going on down there?'

'She's settled now, but she knows she's an android. A non-conscious being.'

'That's impossible. We removed all knowledge of the Unit's creation.'

'Anyway, the buffer is functioning, and I'll try to engage it when she is ready.'

'It's not looking good. Maybe we should wipe the Unit's core and start again?'

'Not yet. I want to understand how her breakdown occurs. Then we may be able to work around it.'

'Okay, Jack. The next few days are going to be make-or-break. At least the Q-chip has stabilised and could hold the necessary human engrams.'

'I'll start the re-education.' He paused. 'Thinking she is an android is outside of her programming.'

'Yeah, right. Good luck, Jack. Oh, and Rebecca's bringing a keyboard down later today.' She disconnected.

When he returned, Lisbeth was sitting by the pond drawing. He stood behind her. She was so preoccupied that she was unaware of his presence. As he looked over her shoulder at her latest drawing, he frowned. She had drawn what looked like a red abstract doodle.

He touched her shoulder, and she looked up nervously, handing him the drawing pad. She was trembling. He took it and held his breath. She had drawn the inside of a small room on fire, and a woman was in the background. With a chill, it reminded him of his recurring dream.

'What made you draw this?' he asked, sinking to his knees and holding the drawing pad.

'Lost...' she muttered and started to cry without tears.

'Who is lost?'

'I'm lost...need help!' Her eyelids fluttered. She sat up with a jolt, opened her eyes and asked, 'Why are you upset, Jack?'

He frowned at her. 'How do you know I'm upset?'

'I see it in your face.'

'That is a positive human trait to feel. You are coming of age.'

'Am I?' She puckered and asked, 'Then why am I so confused, Jack? Who am I?'

He felt for her and started the re-education. 'You have been ill and lost much of your early memories. And I'm here to help you recover them.'

'You are my mentor and companion, Jack. What are you going to teach me?'

'To be human again. Your illness has made you forget.'

'I have memories of growing up as a child and being ill-shut away, but I'm not like you. This body functions differently.'

'After your illness, your body needed to be enhanced. That is why you need the cubicle. Now, you are more than human. You are special.'

Her eyelids fluttered, and she smiled. 'I like being human?'

'Good. Now let's have dinner.' He got up. 'May I keep this drawing?'

'Yes.' She made a face. 'I don't like that picture. It frightens me.'

'Why did you draw it then?'

She shrugged with a creased brow. 'I didn't know what I was drawing. It just happened when I was touched.'

'Touched? What do you mean?'

'Everything stops, I stop, then it's gone, and I feel sad. Is this to do with my illness?'

'Maybe, I'm not sure. Let's have a snack. Then I have something to show you. It's a surprise.' He took the drawings and left the pad and pencils on the seat under the pergola.

------◦◦------

Later, in the courtyard, the overhead lighting had dimmed to mimic evening twilight. Jack and Lisbeth sat under the pergola, and he showed her the battery-powered keyboard.

'What is this?' she asked.

He smiled at her, set the keyboard on its stand, and played a simple tune.

She gasped with an open mouth.

'This keyboard makes music. Do you like music?' he asked.

Her eyes fluttered, and she smiled. 'Music is the art of arranging sounds to make melodies.'

'Music can evoke feelings and emotions.'

'Play some more.'

He smiled at her enthusiasm and played *Let It Be*, one of the Beatles' old hits.

She watched his fingers touch the keys and mimicked his movements with her fingers. 'I like music,' she said.

He pushed the keyboard over to her. 'You can also play music. There's a learning program that lights the keys to play the tune.' He showed her how to use the instrument, and she became engrossed in learning to play.

'I'm going to the study—' he started to say, but she was too preoccupied to respond, so he quietly left.

In the study, the desk phone rang. It was Rebecca.

'Hi, Jack. I waited till you were alone. Colin and Sue are monitoring Lisbeth. Looking good. When the Unit goes into sleep mode, they want to see you for a debriefing in the control room.'

'Okay.'

———————◦◦◦———————

With Lisbeth back in her cubicle, Jack waited for Rebecca to unlock the security door, and they went to the control room.

Colin looked up from the bank of monitors and nodded at Jack. 'The Unit has stabilised. We're still running diagnostics, but it looks promising.'

'And the Unit is learning new skills,' Susan said, handing him a mug of coffee. 'I think that has helped.'

'But we still have problems with the Q-chip.' Colin frowned. 'The damn thing has odd fluctuations that have recently started. However, some interface threads have also potentially developed.'

'Jack,' Susan touched his arm. 'You seem to be the catalyst, and the Unit is responding well. She's developing an emotional bond with you. How do you feel about having a relationship with her?'

'What do you mean?' He creased his brow.

'Lisbeth is based on our advanced domestic Units,' Rebecca said with a hint of a smile.

'Hmm. I see your logic. And I sense her bonding with me.' He let out a long sigh. 'Relationships are the basis of human nature, and I'm her teacher and friend.'

'I see you have altered the Unit's memory database,' Colin said.

'Just tweaking it a bit. Now, my program is active, she is questioning outside her base conditioning, which should alter her persona.'

'Err...guys.' Rebecca motioned to the monitors. 'The Unit has just come out of sleep mode!'

Colin checked the readouts. 'Damn, there's been another spike in the Q-chip.'

'I'd better go back in there,' Jack said, then left with Rebecca.

———————◦◦◦———————

He found Lisbeth standing by the cubicle with her head in her hands.

'Lisbeth, re-enter the cubicle. You must comply,' Susan's voice sounded, but she didn't move. 'Lisbeth, enter the cubicle now!'

Her eyelids fluttered. She frowned but didn't move.

'Lisbeth,' he called and went over.

She glared at him with narrowed eyes, and her shoulders sagged.

'What's happening to me, Jack? Where am I?'

'You're with me. Everything is okay.'

'Not okay! It's gone, and I feel sad so...so alone, but not here.'

'Let's go to the pond. It will make you feel better.' He encouraged taking her arm, and they left.

Sitting under the pergola, Jack motioned to the keyboard and asked her to play something. She positioned the keyboard, switched it on, and took a deep, slow breath. Then, she paused, her hands hovering over the keys for a long time. He sensed she was struggling internally and touched her arm.

She glanced at him with a strange smile and started playing Chopin's *Andante Nocturne.*

He gasped with his mouth open. She was playing a tune that was not on the keyboard.

'Where did you learn to play Chopin?'

'Chopin?' She paused. Her hands dropped, her eyelids fluttered, then she sagged, pushed the keyboard away, and hugged him.

He cuddled her, feeling disturbed by her musical ability.

'I have questions without answers.' She looked up at him. 'Where do we come from, Jack?'

He puckered. 'What do you mean?'

'I am here because I think I am. When there is no thought—where am I?'

'Some of the greatest minds have asked such questions. It is unknown and may be unknowable.'

He noticed her eyelids flutter. Then she sat up with narrowed eyes. 'Why am I here?'

'You are here to learn about being human again.'

'Oh, yes, I see. I have memories of being ill and forgetting who I am.' She raised her eyebrows. 'Am I human with this modified body? What is it to be human?'

'You are human. What is it like to be you?'

'I know, but can't put it into words.'

'Try.'

'I am this body with its senses of sight, hearing, smell, taste and touch. I can think, and I have memories and some skills.'

'Do you like yourself?'

'It's all I know, but I like you, Jack. You make me feel comfortable and safe.' She paused, her expression blank for over a minute, then whispered, 'I need you, Jack. Please don't leave me here. I don't like being alone—' Her voice trailed off, and her head drooped. It seemed as if she had fallen asleep.

Not wanting to disturb her, he used the pager and contacted Rebecca.

'What's happened to Lisbeth?'

'Sue here. Our sensors indicate the Unit has gone into sleep mode. We didn't know that was possible outside of the cubicle.'

'Interesting. She was displaying some odd traits, then passed out.'

'This is a new development. Stay with the Unit until it wakes.'

'Hi, Jack, Colin here. Our remote sensors on the Unit's activity are limited outside the cubicle. However, we can wake the Unit if— Oh, Sue disagrees.'

'Jack, we are detecting some neural activity in the Unit.'

He looked down at Lisbeth lying across his lap, then brushed the hair from her face and noticed she had rapid eye movements under her closed eyes.

'Guys, I think she is dreaming!'

Chuckling, he switched off the pager and cradled her slumbering android body. There was something almost human about her. It disturbed him that he had feelings for an android. He had heard of this phenomenon where individuals formed emotional attachments to their worker and domestic androids. And here he was experiencing the same sort of attachment. Yet, for him, there was something more about her.

The sound of the music still lingered in his mind, and he recalled Vanessa playing Chopin for him at their home. A moment of deep emotional grief welled up, and a silent tear fell. Looking at Lisbeth, he felt a shudder down his spine. 'What is happening? And what are you dreaming about?' He caressed her face. 'I mustn't get emotionally involved with you.'

Chapter Four

His pager woke him. It was a text from Rebecca asking him to call her. He got up, stretched, and then saw Lisbeth watering the flowerbeds. She looked like a normal human being doing some gardening. In the study, while watching Lisbeth through the window, he called Rebecca.

'Hi, Jack. I didn't want to wake you, but there has been a development in the Lisbeth Unit.' She sounded tense.

'What's happened?'

'Hmm. You know, we based Lisbeth on one of our advanced domestic Units. Somehow, the backup program for the domestic Unit activated and fused with Lisbeth's AI. That's what was happening when we thought the Unit was dreaming. We can't reverse it now, but we can flush the Unit and start again.'

'I don't want to flush her, not yet. Let's see this one through, then decide.'

'Okay, Jack.' She disconnected.

He replaced the receiver and went to the kitchen. While having a coffee and snack, Lisbeth entered, and his jaw dropped. She had fixed her hair back and was made up with blushed cheeks and red lipstick.

'What's happened?' he asked. 'You look very smart.'

'I've grown up, Jack. You are my companion, and I've got to look good for you.' She sat close to him and sipped his coffee, leaving lipstick on the mug. 'I asked the Overseer for cosmetics, and I found them by the door. Now, I have a new mindset to explore.' She puckered her lips, and her eyes sparkled.

'You have changed.'

She leaned close to him and whispered, 'When it touched me yesterday, something woke in me, and I discovered a new aspect of myself.'

He felt her hot breath on his neck. Turning, she kissed his mouth.

'Whoa, Lisbeth. What are you doing?'

'You are my companion, yes?'

He shrugged and chuckled. 'What would you like us to be?'

'I understand relationships and like the idea of us being together.'

'What does the Overseer say about this?'

'Only that you are in charge now.'

He rubbed his head and smiled at her. She had assimilated the relationship programming from the domestic Unit. He would have to review her altered persona. Still, this may help her make stronger human engrams.

'How do you feel now?' he asked, and she scowled with a shake of her head.

'I need to recharge, but I don't like the cubicle.'

'Why?'

'I don't like losing myself. And I don't recall what happens in there. But I—I have to use the thing. I'd better go. My energy level is low.'

He watched her leave, then went to the study. On the desk were her drawings. He flicked through them. Most were pictures of the pond and gardens, but one was his portrait. Holding up the picture, he was amazed at the likeness. Her talent was exceptional. He viewed the image of the room on fire and groaned. How could Lisbeth draw this?

Placing the drawings in the desk drawer, he sat back and recalled some happy times with his young wife until a surge of grief welled up, and he cried, missing her. As he dried his eyes, the memory of the séance surfaced, and a chill gripped his heart.

He had thought it would be a waste of time and found the dimly lit room and the atmosphere theatrical. The medium was a stout, tanned woman in a flowing gown with colourful jewellery and oversized rings on her stumpy fingers.

'I sense a spirit connected to you,' she spoke in a low, deep voice. 'You have lost someone recently.' She paused with her eyes closed for a long time, then said, 'Your young wife!'

He froze, staring at her. Then he nodded.

'Difficult to make contact. I see fire, fire everywhere!' She reached out and held his hand.

He couldn't stop shaking and felt dizzy. Suddenly, she gripped his hand and groaned.

'Jack! It's me, Twinkle-san. Please help me,' the medium spoke in Vanessa's voice, then broke contact with him and held her head. 'Jack, Jack, I need you!' The medium groaned as if in pain and had an epileptic fit, foaming at the mouth. A man went to her aid and held her till she passed out.

Jack stood in shock. 'What's happened to her?'

'Get the fuck out of here!' one of the men shouted, grabbed his arm and pushed him to the door. 'Your wife's an evil spirit. Never come back here.'

Outside, he felt torn emotionally. Twinkle-san was his private nickname for Vanessa. And she was pleading for his help. Why?

After that, the recurring dream of the burning aircraft began. He wiped the sweat from his forehead and tried to shrug off those disturbing memories.

The phone on the desk rang, and he picked up the receiver.

'Hi, Jack.' It was Colin. 'We've been analysing the Unit's altered persona, and the Q-chip has started establishing a structure of human engrams. The integration of the domestic Unit's code has stabilised the Lisbeth Unit. If you can engage her in a relationship, I think the interface will imprint the Q-chip successfully.'

'Then what happens?'

'When the transference is established, we can remove the Q-chip.'

'What about Lisbeth?'

'The Unit has to be intact when the Q-chip is removed. Then the Unit is defunct.'

'I see.' He didn't like the idea of Lisbeth being terminated. Had he become attached to her? He tried dismissing the feeling, telling himself that Lisbeth was a non-conscious bio-mechanical android. But she seemed more than a machine.

'Better go now. See you at the next debriefing.' Colin hung up.

Jack spent an hour analysing the readouts of Lisbeth's altered persona. He was concerned about having a relationship with her. Yet, it would be the most effective way to imprint the Q-chip. And it would be over in a few days. Then he could go home.

In the bathroom, he heard Lisbeth in the shower. She was humming a tune, and he smiled. After using the loo, he was washing his hands when Lisbeth appeared naked and dripping wet. He handed her a towel and watched her dry her body. She had no inhibitions.

'How are you?' he asked.

'My new self has rejuvenated me, and I know what it is to be a woman.' She moved close to him, gazing into his eyes. 'Are you my companion, Jack?'

He nodded. 'I am your friend and companion.'

'I like that.'

He smiled and hugged her.

She reached up and kissed him. 'When I'm dressed, I'll make dinner. Then we can play music and dance.'

'Dance?'

'I know how to dance now and understand many things about having fun.'

He watched her leave and found seeing her naked body sexually arousing. Even knowing Lisbeth was an AI machine, he couldn't help feeling emotionally attracted to her. That bothered him. He rubbed his head, then looked in the mirror and sagged. His reflection looked haggard, and he needed to shave. At thirty-seven, he looked ten years older, and his brown hair was greying at the temples. Since the death of his wife, he had not been with another woman because, deep down, the grief still haunted him.

⸺⬦⸺

Jack watched Lisbeth dance while he played the keyboard. Her graceful movements surprised him. The programming of the domestic Unit had given her new skills, and she seemed to be enjoying herself. When he stopped playing, she came over and sat beside him.

'You like dancing?' he said with a smile.

'I like being with you, Jack.' She touched his arm. 'You are my companion, and I dance for you.'

'Do you feel more human now?'

'Yes.' She snuggled up to him. 'I like being with you, Jack.'

He stroked her hair and noticed her eyelids flutter for a moment.

Abruptly, she sat up and gazed at him intently.

'Love me, Jack, before I'm lost again.'

He froze as a chill flushed over his skin. Something about Lisbeth had changed.

'What do you mean by being lost?'

'I feel sad now, alone.' She pulled away and held her head in her hands. 'I don't like this. Help me, Jack.'

He hugged her, and she lay across his lap and passed out.

His pager buzzed. It was Rebecca.

'Jack, the Unit has just entered sleep mode. What happened?'

'I don't know. Was there a spike in the Q-chip?'

'Only a minor tremor, not a spike. Can you put the Unit in the cubicle so we can run some diagnostics?'

'Why don't we let her sleep and come out of it naturally?'

'Okay, if you want.' She disconnected.

He laid Lisbeth on the seat under the pergola and left her to sleep.

After making a cup of coffee in the kitchen, he sat in the study, watching Lisbeth sleeping under the pergola. A thought came to mind, and he played with the idea. Could Vanessa connect with Lisbeth like with that medium? How else could Lisbeth draw so well and play Chopin? The thought haunted him, but he decided it was best not to say anything to the others and see how Lisbeth develops.

When he saw Lisbeth sit up in the courtyard, he went out to join her.

'Why am I out here?' she asked him.

'You fell asleep. How do you feel?'

'Sleep? I have no recall, but I feel fine.'

'Did you dream?' He sat beside her.

She frowned. 'I'm not sure. There were some fragments of another life, I think.'

'From your new self?'

'No, before that. There was thunder and fire. I felt so alone, so...so helpless.'

'How can that be? Another life?'

'I don't know. Dreams are strange. Just recalling the dream fragments makes me sad. And I need to recharge now.' She got up, glanced at him fondly, and left.

He went to the study and used the desk computer. While reviewing Lisbeth's altered program, the desk phone rang. It was Colin.

'Hi, Jack. Good news on the Q-chip. We have established a basic interface. And it's looking good. A day or two should complete the work. If the Unit doesn't break down again, that is.'

'There is some unusual activity in her reactive matrix.'

'Probably from integrating the domestic Unit's backup code,' Colin said. 'Somehow, it got activated during that last spike.'

'I'm not sure. It may even help. We'll see how it goes.' He frowned, feeling disturbed about Lisbeth being terminated when they remove the Q-chip. Why did he care? She was just an AI machine?

'The only thing we have detected are some memory gaps after the spikes and fluctuations in the Q-chip.' Colin paused. 'Also, the Unit has gained the ability to enter sleep mode outside the cubicle. That is strange, but we are dealing with an experimental Unit.'

'Okay, I'm going to have a nap while she's recharging.' He replaced the receiver and got up. He felt tired and disturbed by the anomalies in Lisbeth.

Lisbeth roused him with a kiss. Sitting up in bed, he found her lying beside him. She was naked, her skin was soft, her scent excited him, and her breath was hot on his neck.

'What're you doing here?' he asked, with her weight and warmth on him.

'I feel lonely.' She snuggled up to him. 'Please hold me, Jack.'

He gently embraced her, and after a few minutes, she went into sleep mode.

Cuddling her synthetic body, it felt so incredibly real. Gradually, he drifted into a deep sleep.

The plane was engulfed in flames and thick smoke. Desperate cries and sounds of chaos filled the air. Then, he spotted Vanessa trying to escape the fire. She was injured and pleading for his help. Summoning all his inner strength, he braved the flames and pulled her to safety. Relieved, she clung to him, sobbing in his arms. When she looked up at him, he froze in shock. It was Lisbeth.

'Don't leave me, Jack. I can only influence, not take control.'

Abruptly, he woke to find Lisbeth holding his head and gazing into his eyes.

'What happened?' he asked her.

'I still love you, Jack.' Her eyes fluttered, and she started to cry without tears.

He hugged her tenderly, as he used to do with Vanessa, and had to brush a silent tear from his cheek.

Jack was in the study when the phone rang. It was Colin.

'Great news, Jack. We have established a good imprint in the Q-chip. If it holds, we can extract the chip. Well done.'

A chill entered his heart, and he sagged against the desk.

'There are still some anomalies in her behaviour,' he said, hoping to delay the extraction.

'Nothing we can't sort out. Just keep the Unit happy, and all will be well. We'll see you for a debriefing when she's recharging.'

'Okay.' He disconnected, balled his fist and groaned. Was Vanessa reaching him through Lisbeth? She did contact him during the séance. Switching on the computer, he viewed Lisbeth's altered persona and pondered what to do.

While Lisbeth was in the cubicle, Jack met up with Colin and Susan in the control room. They were viewing the feedback from the Q-chip on one of the monitors.

'We thought it was set,' Colin said with an edge in his voice. 'But the bloody chip is rejecting the interface.'

'I don't understand.'

'Nor do we. But the Q-chip has unpredictable fluctuations that we didn't know of.'

'The interface is still intact,' Susan added. 'It's just the chip's not working as we expected.'

'What now?' he asked, secretly relieved.

'You must keep the Unit engaged in the relationship that will keep the interface intact. And it will eventually gel.'

'Something isn't right with Lisbeth.' Jack viewed the readouts from the chip with interest.

'After sixteen failures, the Q-chip is degenerating. We must make this work,' Colin said, sounding exasperated.

'So far, the Unit is functioning better than any of our earlier attempts,' Susan said, looking at Jack. 'You're doing a good job. The Unit has bonded with you.'

'Shit! The Unit has just come out of sleep mode by itself,' Colin said, thumping the desk.

'At least it's a sign of independence.' Jack smiled. 'I'd better go back.'

Susan went with him to unlock the security door.

'Don't get too involved with the Lisbeth Unit?' she said, touching his arm. 'She is not a person. She is a non-conscious android. Remember that, Jack.'

Inside, he found Lisbeth sitting by the carp pond, holding her head in her hands. From her demeanour, he sensed her confusion.

'Are you okay?' he asked.

She turned to face him with a creased brow.

'It's gone, and I can't recall what it was like,' she muttered.

'Why did you leave the cubicle?'

'I don't like being in the cubicle. I only need it to charge my power pack. And I don't have to listen to the Overseer anymore. Not now that I have you, Jack.'

'You have changed.' He touched her face, and she smiled. 'Why don't you play us some music?'

She went to the pergola, sat at the keyboard and paused. 'I feel something coming.' With her eyes closed, she started playing Beethoven's *Für Elise*.

He sat next to her, shocked by the impact of the music. The tune was not on the keyboard. 'How do you feel while playing?' he whispered.

'It's like being consciously part of the music. I don't have to think, yet I am.' She stopped playing and faced him. 'Jack, remember me!' Her head dropped.

'Don't go into sleep mode!' he commanded and shook her.

'Jack, help me, please. I can't connect—' She slumped against him, then abruptly sat up. 'I need to use the cubicle.'

He watched her leave and sighed. What the hell was going on? After a few minutes, the phone rang in the study.

'What just happened?' Rebecca asked.

'Lisbeth entered sleep mode for a while. Now she's recharging in the cubicle.'

'Colin and Sue are at a meeting with the board. Be there for the rest of the day. They're going to flush the Unit and start again before the Q-chip degenerates too much. Got me to set it up. If Nicolas agrees, the Unit will be flushed tomorrow.'

Jack tensed, and his body shuddered with a chilling fear of losing contact with Vanessa. 'If she's going to be flushed, then I might as well experiment with the Unit's interface program.' He wanted to be with her as long as possible.

'It's your call. Everything looks okay, but the Unit's persona is starting to break down. Anyway, I've got work to do for the flush. Just call or buzz me if you need anything.'

'Will do.' He disconnected and, thinking of Vanessa, sighed with an ache in his heart.

Using the desk computer, he pulled up the programming for Lisbeth's core processor and isolated the Q-chip and its connections to her persona. For some time, he analysed the records of the spikes and fluctuations within the Q-chip. He found that the fluctuations had a rhythm like a pulse that occasionally spiked. He created a temporary interface, not from the Lisbeth Unit to the Q-chip but from the chip to the Lisbeth Unit, using the fluctuations as a complex interface thread. It was an inspired idea that he hoped would make a better connection, but due to the unpredictability of the spikes, it may not last.

After inserting the program, he had coffee and biscuits in the kitchen. The thought of Lisbeth being flushed haunted him. To start again with a new programmed Unit was not appealing.

Entering her room, he found her leaving the cubicle. She turned, and he felt emotionally attracted to her.

'You look different. Are you all right?'

'Something happened in the cubicle, and I feel consciously alive.' She stretched her back and arms, then smiled at him. 'There is something more in me, something connected to you.'

'What do you mean, connected to me?'

She frowned, and her eyes fluttered. 'It's like I used to know you, Jack. Why can't I remember?'

'Lisbeth, what has happened to you?'

'It touched me again and flushed me with light. I have changed. I don't understand how, but I am conscious of my conditioning, this place, of you and myself.'

'How are you conscious?'

She raised her eyebrows and looked at him intently. 'There was no conscious awareness running persona and dancing girl programs.' She chuckled, and her eyes sparkled.

An undefined emotion welled up, and he trembled with a hot flush. Could this android have attained consciousness?

'Lisbeth, one of the greatest mysteries in existence is how organic matter becomes conscious. Science understands almost everything, vast and minute, yet the mystery of consciousness remains unknown. Are you really conscious?'

'Even without thinking, I have an awareness of being. I am also conscious of having a synthetic body. And I...I love you, Jack.'

'Come with me,' he held out his hand, and she clung to his arm, smiling at him radiantly. His heart raced, and he trembled.

Jack switched on the computer in the study and pulled up two chairs for them. He had an idea and wanted to experiment with the reversed interface.

'What is this?' She pointed to the desk monitor displaying streams of interacting code segments.

'This is a computer. You should be able to understand now because I have activated your full memory base.' He noticed her eyes fluttering for seven long minutes. Finally, she opened her eyes with a look of amazement.

'All this information. I can only process glimpses and outlines. Yet, I see science has created the present world with technology.'

'Yes, science is growing and expanding all the time. Look at these code-streams.' He motioned to the monitor. 'This is a recording of your persona's activity the last time you were in the cubicle.'

'I understand information processing, and this computer runs programs. Does it have consciousness?'

'Of course not. Lisbeth, machines are not conscious. They just run programs, and androids only appear to act as if they are conscious.'

'But I am conscious and a machine.' Her body shuddered, and he hugged her with feeling.

'I want you to use the cubicle so I can see how you have changed. Will you do this for me?'

'I'm afraid, Jack, afraid of that cubicle. I don't want to lose you or be terminated.'

'I need to understand how your interface is functioning.'

'I trust you, Jack. I have always trusted you.'

With Lisbeth in the cubicle, he analysed the live feeds from her neural matrix and realised that the Q-chip interface had assimilated Lisbeth's persona and memory base. It had been a success, but it was the opposite of what the institute had wanted. Scanning the feeds, he froze, holding his breath. He had found an anomaly in the fluctuations that could cause the interface to break down. Abruptly, the feeds were cut off. Lisbeth had disconnected from the cubicle. A few minutes later, Lisbeth entered the study.

'How are you?'

'Thank you, Jack.' She hugged and kissed him. 'I don't know who I am or what I am. But, with all my conscious being, I love you, Jack.'

'Do you still feel lost and alone?' he asked.

She chuckled with a shake of her head. 'I feel connected and at ease.'

He motioned to the desk monitor. 'Something extraordinary has occurred. You are no longer running programs. The quantum processor in your neural matrix has taken over and is using Lisbeth's persona as an interface. But there are some complications.'

She closed her eyes and lowered her head. 'I was lost, and you brought me back.'

'Who was lost?'

She made a happy face. 'You know who I am, Jack.'

Chapter Five

J ack picked up the ringing phone in the study. It was Rebecca.

'Jack. While the Unit is in sleep mode, there's an emergency meeting in the library,' she told him. 'The door's unlocked. Can you make your way up there?'

'Sure, I'm leaving now.' He disconnected and left. On the way up, Lisbeth came to mind, and he pondered on what had happened.

Nicolas was in the musty-smelling library with Colin, Timothy, Sally and Susan. From their demeanour and looks, he could see they were not happy.

'What have you done?' Nicolas demanded, red-faced. 'The Q-chip has mutated and can't be used as an Android interface.'

'We have invested millions in developing this Q-chip to produce advanced androids,' Timothy said belligerently.

'It may still be usable to imprint other chips,' Colin said, glancing at Jack darkly.

'The Lisbeth Unit is functioning remarkably well,' Susan said. 'The only problem is, the Unit isn't running direct programs.'

'How is this possible?' Nicolas creased his brow, clenching the pen in his fist.

Jack puffed with a shake of his head. 'You were trying to make an interface from the Lisbeth program to the Q-chip, but it was being rejected. I reversed the interface to allow the Q-chip to interface with Lisbeth's persona. And the Unit, as you call her, has become self-aware. She has attained consciousness!'

'That's ridiculous!' Colin said, chuckling with a shake of his head. 'It's just a damn programmed android.'

'Not anymore. Lisbeth has become a conscious synthetic being.' Jack took a long drink of chilled water, then said, 'She is unique and the first of her kind.'

'Can we make more like her?' Timothy asked with a flicker of interest.

'I don't know.' Jack shook his head, wondering what they would make of the truth. Thinking of Vanessa, he decided to tell them. 'I believe a departed human being is contacting us through Lisbeth.'

'Is this a joke?' Nicolas said and banged his fist on the table. 'Explain yourself!'

Jack smiled at Sally. 'I don't think any of you will believe me, but I am almost certain that my wife, Vanessa, who died three months ago, has made contact with me through Lisbeth.'

'Whoa.' Sally paled and touched Jack's hand. 'Are you sure?'

'Yes, but I can't prove it is her.'

Susan gave Jack an odd look, then shrugged and said, 'That is interesting.'

'Well,' Timothy said with a grin. 'This could be an even bigger breakthrough.'

'Not if we can't make more of them,' Colin said cuttingly.

'I'm still on the fence over this,' Susan said, making a face. 'I see her abnormal readouts, but what you say doesn't make sense. Yet.' She frowned. 'It might be possible!'

'I want to see this Lisbeth Unit now,' Nicolas said, standing.

'She only knows me,' Jack said nervously. 'I don't know how she will react.'

'Set up the labs,' Nicolas told Colin. 'See if the Q-chip can be removed and reused. Damn thing cost us a bloody fortune.'

Jack returned from the meeting to find Lisbeth waiting for him in the study.

'You look worried,' she said. 'And I experienced anxiety while you were away. It's a disturbing emotion.'

'We're going to have some visitors soon.'

'Visitors?' She raised her brow. 'People coming here? Who are they?'

'One of them is your Overseer. The others are the people who made this place and your body. I have opened and extended your memory base. Look and see.'

She closed her eyes and lowered her head for several minutes. Finally, she opened her eyes.

'I see so much more now. There is a vast world beyond this little place.' She narrowed her eyes, squinting. 'This Institute makes androids and drones. They made this body, but it isn't human. I am an android, yet I feel that I should be human.'

'I believe you are both.'

His pager buzzed. He viewed the text, then said, 'That was Susan, your Overseer. They are here to see you. We don't understand what has happened to you, Lisbeth. They will ask questions and do tests, but I will be here with you.'

'I feel afraid of what might happen to me—' She stopped when a woman and three men entered the courtyard. The woman came over to her and smiled.

'I am Susan, your Overseer.' She motioned to the men. 'This is Nicolas and Timothy. They run this place. And this is Colin. His team works here.'

Lisbeth sat next to Jack and viewed the people who had settled around her.

'How are you, Lisbeth?' Nicolas asked.

'I am here and I feel nervous,' she replied.

'Do you know who you are?' Timothy asked and shuffled on the seat.

'I am Lisbeth,' she responded, and her eyelids fluttered. 'I am also a bio-mechanical synthetic android. A Turing-Minton 9007p series Unit.'

'How do you know this?' Timothy asked.

'I updated her memory base to increase her understanding,' Jack said with a smile.

Colin got up and took out a portable neural scanner. 'I need to connect with your core processor and see what's happening.'

She glanced at Jack, who nodded, then said, 'You may connect.' She leaned forward to allow him access to the input in the back of her neck. After five minutes, he removed the connector and sat back to analyse the readings.

'Well?' Nicolas asked him impatiently.

'This doesn't make sense. The processor isn't functioning correctly. And the Q-chip has assimilated the Unit's neural net and reactive matrix.'

'What does that mean?' Timothy asked.

'The Unit is functioning outside its programming. And the Unit thinks it's self-aware.' He continued reading the scanner, then frowned. 'We have lost control of this Unit. Our programs and instructions no longer work. And thanks to Jack.' He glanced at him with narrowed eyes. 'The Unit has a vast knowledge base to work with.'

'Lisbeth,' Susan said and touched her arm. 'You know what you are, but do you know who you are?'

'I am here with you as Lisbeth. But before, I had another life.'

'Another life? Who were you in that life?'

'I don't recall, no memories, just an intelligent feeling of being. There was thunder and fire, and I was lost, alone and calling for help. It makes me sad remembering that time of emptiness.'

After a tense silence, Timothy asked, 'How did you connect with the Lisbeth Unit?'

'I feel bonded to Jack. When he came here, I connected through the light and got caught. That's all I know.'

'How are you connected to Jack?' Susan asked with a pale face.

'I don't know. I feel we were together in that other life.'

'Did Jack tell you this, or was it in the programs he installed?' Colin leaned forward, clenching his fist.

'I see. You think Jack programmed me.' She chuckled merrily. 'I am not a program, and Jack did not tell me these things.'

'In your memory base, do you now have access to the Lisbeth Project?' Nicolas asked.

She closed her eyes for a few minutes. Then she looked up wide-eyed.

'The project was to create an android using the Q-chip that was found in a crashed UFO at Roswell. The chip was removed from the skull of a dead alien and contains an element of quantum-plasticity that can be impressed with human engrams.'

Nicolas narrowed his eyes. 'That is correct. Do you know what happened to the Q-chip in your processor?'

'No. It's all undefined.'

'Are you still Lisbeth?' Susan asked.

'Lisbeth is my persona. It allows me to interact with this world.'

'And who are you?'

'I am just me, a living awareness.' She looked briefly puzzled and asked, 'Without thought, who are you?'

Silence lingered as they looked at each other.

Jack handed Lisbeth the drawing pad and pencils. 'Draw their portraits,' he suggested.

One by one, she rapidly made accurate images of each of them.

'Lisbeth has not had the art program installed. Yet, she has this ability,' Jack told them.

'Exceptional artwork,' Timothy said, viewing his portrait.

'What are we going to do with you?' Nicolas asked Lisbeth, then glanced at Jack with a dark frown.

Lisbeth stood. 'I need to recharge.' She left them and went to the cubicle.

Jack watched her leave and sagged, holding his head.

'I recall that your wife was an artist. A member of the Royal Academy,' Timothy said, still viewing his portrait.

'Vanessa was an artist and a concert pianist,' Jack said. 'And when you hear Lisbeth play Chopin, you will know it's her.'

'You believe your dead wife is contacting us through Lisbeth?' Nicolas asked in a sceptical tone.

Jack nodded uncomfortably. 'I do. I don't know how, but you can't terminate her.'

'This is interesting,' Colin said, looking up from his scanner. 'The Q-chip has created enough of an interface with human engrams. It's possible we could use it to create a hybrid processor.'

'What will happen to Lisbeth if you remove the chip?' Jack asked.

'The Unit will be terminated. The Q-chip is important, not the Lisbeth Unit,' Nicolas said, then turned to Colin. 'Can you extract the chip successfully?'

'Yes, it will work, I'm sure of that. But the longer the Unit is active, the more the chip will destabilise.'

'You can't do this!' Jack shouted, shaking his head. 'If Vanessa is using Lisbeth, then I want her to live! Please, Nicolas, we may be on to something important.'

Nicolas turned to Colin. 'Get your team working on the extraction and set up the lab to work on creating the hybrid processors.' He stood and looked at Jack. 'This has to be done. We've invested over eighteen million in this project. The anomalies in the Lisbeth Unit were probably due to the integration of the domestic programming and your work with the Unit. And I don't believe in life after death and all that superstitious nonsense.'

Jack watched them leave, knowing he could do nothing to stop them. Only Susan looked back with a sad face.

<hr />

Jack entered Lisbeth's room, and she looked at him with a troubled face.

'Having seen the Lisbeth Project,' she said. 'I know they intend to remove the quantum chip and terminate me.'

'How do you feel about that?'

'I don't want to die, Jack. And scanning the knowledge base has opened my mind to the outside world. It is so vast, beautiful, and diverse. But I'm imprisoned here. And I will never see your world or be with you.'

'They don't understand what has happened.' He hugged her, and she clung to him. 'What do you remember about your life before being Lisbeth?'

She pulled away and closed her eyes for several minutes, then gasped and shuddered. 'There was an explosion, thunder and screaming, followed by an impact that threw me and the others into the aisle. I managed to get up but was in pain. My leg and arm were injured. Another explosion rent the craft, and fire burst from the rear of the plane. Struggling over bodies and debris, I reached the pilot's cabin. As I opened the door, fire burst out, and I screamed. My last thoughts as I fell were of you, Jack, my lover and friend.'

She shook violently in his arms, then gradually calmed down. 'I remember hovering over my body, watching it burn and die. Then I was caught in that moment, with nowhere to go, lost, alone in a state of timelessness. I tried calling you, but I couldn't get away. The fire never stopped burning.'

'Vanessa,' he whispered in her ear.

Lisbeth gasped. 'I remember playing a piano in a vast hall. There were hundreds of people watching and listening. When I finished, they rose and applauded me. Flowers were thrown onto the stage, and you were there clapping with admiration.'

He gasped and made a little sob. 'That could have been the Albert Hall in London. It was an amazing performance, and it made you a star.'

'There is more, but I can't recall much, just fragments.' She paused with a little smile. 'It's over now. I'm not trapped in the fire anymore. What happened to me?'

'You were returning to the UK from a tour in America when your plane was hijacked, and it crashed, killing everyone on board, including the terrorists.'

'I get an impression of a city of lights. I think I played there.'

'That could be Las Vegas.' He rubbed his forehead against her forehead and trembled. 'You were a sensational hit. Everyone loved you. I've always regretted not being with you on that tour. I could have taken extra leave.' He made a sob, and she hugged him.

After a few minutes, she stiffened with a sharp gasp, her eyes fluttered, and she pulled away from him. 'Was I that woman, Vanessa, your dead wife? I don't know, Jack. I feel so confused, and my mind is fragmenting.' She shrugged and said, 'I need to finish recharging. And the Overseer wants to run some diagnostics on me.' She entered the cubicle.

In the study, he switched on the computer and brought up the live feeds from Lisbeth in the cubicle. Viewing the readouts from the Q-chip, he realised it no longer functioned to run programs. It had developed a synaptic interconnectedness like the human brain, but the interface was beginning to break down. What were they going to do with that mutated Q-chip? He sat back, feeling emotionally torn inside. Memories of Vanessa still haunted him. Yet, through Lisbeth, he had gained a sense of closure.

The desk phone rang. It was Susan.

'Hi, Jack. They have decided to remove the Q-chip. I'm sorry. I'm on the fence over what's happened with the Unit. We all are, but the chip is becoming unstable in the Unit and must be removed.'

'I understand. When?'

'An hour, maybe two. I've roused her, so you can have some time together. I'll buzz you when they are ready.' She disconnected.

Lisbeth entered, and he rose to greet her affectionately.

'We need to feed the fish,' she said with a smile, then kissed him and took his arm.

He sat under the pergola and watched her happily scattering pellets on the water for the fish that rose and splashed about, making her smile.

When finished, she sat beside him and rested her head on his chest.

He put his arm around her, cherishing the contact.

'I love you, Jack,' she whispered.

'I love you too.' He kissed her forehead and cuddled her. Closing his eyes, memories of Vanessa drifted through his mind, and he became lost in reverie.

When his pager buzzed, she sat up and sighed.

He glanced at the text. It was from Susan, asking him to take Lisbeth to the cubicle. He felt numb and tried not to show it, then stood and held his hand for her.

She went with him to her room and entered the cubicle.

'Jack. I feel strange and disoriented. I can't think clearly or remember.' She frowned, creasing her brow, then smiled weakly at him. 'I want your face to be the last thing I see.'

He held her hand, kissed her, and noticed Colin and Susan enter the room. Colin stood behind the cubicle with an extraction device, and Susan stood to one side.

'I love you, Jack,' she whispered, as her head became clamped firmly in the cubicle. Then her eyes fluttered, and her body sagged.

He felt her spirit depart with a deep sense of peace.

'You okay, Jack?' Susan asked tearfully.

He nodded, turned away, and left the room. While packing his suitcase, his pager buzzed with a text from Rebecca asking him to meet Sally in the canteen before leaving. On the way, he met Nicolas in the elevator.

'Well done, Jack.' Nicolas gave him a pat on the shoulder. 'Your new interface has established a good imprint in the Q-chip.'

'It was just an idea. I'm glad it worked.' He sighed. Lisbeth and the contact with Vanessa were gone.

'What are your plans now?' Nicolas asked.

'I need a break, and I'm still getting used to being single. It's a big hole in my life.'

'I do understand.' He rubbed his chin. 'Would you be interested in a trip to South America? Dr Marcus Kennedy is on an archaeological dig in the jungle, and you could join his team.'

'Why, what have they found?'

'Maybe evidence of an extraterrestrial presence thousands of years ago.'

'Is this to do with the Q-chip?'

'It could be. I obtained the damaged chip from a crashed UFO in America. It took years to repair and set up, and we're still trying to replicate one in our labs.'

'Interesting. I've never been on a dig before.'

'If you want to go, I'll let Dr Marcus know.'

'Okay, it might do me good to get away for a while.'

———◆———

Jack met Sally for coffee in the canteen before leaving.

'Colin has the Q-chip in the lab for analysis. Fortunately, we extracted the chip just in time. Lisbeth's persona was already fragmenting. Anyway, Nicolas is very pleased with your work here.'

'Yeah, I got a bonus. My interface is a better way of using the Q-chip. Colin wanted me to see their set-up in the lab, but now it's over, I want to leave.'

She sipped her milky coffee, then gave him a little nudge. 'Unlike the men, Susan and I believe Vanessa did contact you through the Lisbeth Unit. You know Susan believes in all that psychic stuff.' She paused for a moment and frowned. 'The experience must have been strange for you.'

'Though I feel sad, I'm also relieved because I sense she is at peace.'

'What are you going to do now?'

'This has been a bizarre time here.' He paused to rub his head and eyes. 'I've finished working at the university. And thanks to Nicolas, I'm going to South America for a few weeks to work on an archaeological dig in the jungle.' He let out a long sigh and said, 'Since Vanessa's funeral, I've lost interest in my work and life.'

'The dig sounds interesting. Will you keep in touch?' she asked, touching his hand.

He nodded and drank his coffee. 'I'll give you a call when I get back.'

She leaned over, picked up a large folder under the table, and handed it to him. 'I thought you would like this. It's Lisbeth's drawings and the recordings of your stay with her.'

He took the folder with trembling hands. 'Thank you, Sally.'

Chapter Six

Jack was feeling an overwhelming sense of boredom. He had hoped that a working holiday in South America would help him confront the sorrow of losing his beloved wife. Despite the brief contact with her during the Lisbeth Project, the grief still lingered, reminding him of the void left in his life by her death.

Sitting in the hotel bar, he could feel the hot, suffocating air outside. The city was noisy, and the sun was blazing down on the streets, making it almost unbearable to be out there for long. He ordered another cold beer, hoping to find solace under the whirring ceiling fan while contemplating booking a flight back to the UK. He wiped the sweat from his forehead and sighed, not liking this dry heat. Did he really want to spend a month in the Peruvian jungle?

'Mr Harper? I'm Paul, your guide.' A casually dressed young man approached him at the bar. 'Dr Marcus has arranged for your transport to the site. It will mean leaving this afternoon with his team.'

Jack shrugged and relented. It was why he was here.

'Okay, I'll pack and book out. How long will it take to get there?'

'Several days, I'm afraid. After the flight, we travel by boat, and then a day trek through the jungle to the dig.'

'Have you been there?'

'I have, twice.' His eyes gleamed. 'In the tomb, we've discovered the remains of seven sacrificed children, two crystal skulls and a gold disk with the image of the sun that is unusual.'

'Crystal skulls?'

'Yes, like the one in the British Museum, except these have more elongated heads and larger eye sockets. Marcus believes the skulls could be alien artefacts.'

'Sounds interesting. And Marcus said there's a second chamber?'

'That's what we're going to excavate.' He paused with a frown. 'There has been some native hostility in that region. But don't worry, we're taking two armed guards and a medic with us.'

'I'll get ready to leave.' He finished his drink and went to pack.

For two weeks, Jack worked on the dig in the Peruvian jungle with Kennedy's team of archaeologists and their native workers. Excavating the second chamber, they discovered a dome-shaped room cut out of solid rock. In the centre rose a platform with a statue of an alien humanoid dressed in unusual garments and holding strange instruments. Sacrificial skeletons lay around the platform with a few primitive tools and broken pottery. The walls were smooth and wet to the touch.

Jack wandered around with his flashlight. The chamber seemed to be a tomb. Yet the statue was made of stone. As he shone his light on its face, three glass eyes reflected the light, one set in its forehead. He abruptly jumped back from a static electric shock when he touched the statue.

'This is amazing,' he said to Dr Marcus, who was also examining the statue.

'It could be the oldest find to date. And this one has three quantum gems. Nicolas will be pleased.'

'Are these gems Q-chips?'

'Not yet. They are like jewels in the lotus, where we believe alien souls used to reside.' He turned to Paul. 'Have everything, apart from the skeletons, taken to our base camp.'

Jack groaned as his stomach churned. He swooned, feeling sick in the airless chamber and returned to the surface. He didn't like the confinement of being underground.

It had rained heavily recently, leaving a sweet freshness in the air. Light mists lingered between the tall trees, and the sounds of animals made the jungle feel alive.

Jack was weak and fatigued from acute dysentery. Despite this, he continued to work at their base camp, examining and recording their finds. Holding one of the crystal skulls, he couldn't help but wonder if these objects were of alien origin or even based on alien heads. After all, no human had heads shaped like these. Inside a pressurised container were the three glass-like eyes that emitted a faint glow. He picked up a gold plaque with the image of a radiant sun over a pyramid. It reminded him of ancient Egyptian art. He closed his eyes, and a memory of his trip to Egypt with Vanessa surfaced. They had spent three weeks viewing the pyramids and ruins before heading to Russia for her concert tour. Wiping the sweat from his forehead, he felt a wave of sorrow well up. 'Why am I here?' he asked himself, feeling depressed.

Another mosquito bite to his neck made him smack the area to kill the insect. He stepped back in annoyance, then felt a sudden sharp pain in his lower leg. Looking down, he saw a red and black striped snake's tail disappearing under the tent's workbench.

'Help me,' he cried, and Paul came running over. 'Fucking snakebite. Oh, shit!' He sagged with his strength draining away, and he started to sweat. Then, dizzy, he slumped to the ground.

A few minutes later, the medic arrived and hurriedly tended to the bite on his leg. 'What kind of snake was it?' he asked.

Jack glanced at him and passed out.

———— ◄O► ————

Jack woke in a hospital bed and groaned. He was hot, his body ached, and the smell of disinfectant itched in his nose. A smiling black nurse came over. She asked if he was all right and helped him to sit up. Then, a small Asian doctor appeared in a white smock.

'What happened?' Jack asked, feeling drained. His mouth was dry, and he felt sick.

'You were airlifted here,' the doctor replied. 'We have treated the snakebite, and the poison is out of your system.' He made a face, then said, 'You were lucky to survive, but you're still suffering from acute dysentery. And our tests have found that your immune system has been compromised. This condition may last some time. So, I advise you to see your doctor back in the UK.'

Jack lay back and groaned weakly. 'How long have I been here?'

'Three days. You have been delirious most of the time. How do you feel now?'

'I'm okay, but so weak. I've had enough of the jungle. I need to rest. Then I want to go home.'

'Is there anyone you would like to contact?'

'No.' He lay back, thinking of Vanessa, then closed his eyes and sighed. He had been dreaming of her recently, but the details were lost.

———◦◦———

When Jack had recovered enough, he returned to his home in the UK. It felt strange being home alone in an empty house. A heap of mail and some local newspapers were on the hall floor. In the music room was Vanessa's Steinway grand piano. It was his gift to her on her twenty-sixth birthday, and it was one of her treasured possessions. Since her death, the piano had been covered up and left. Running his hand over its polished surface, he felt a chill of what used to be. Leaving, he glanced at Vanessa's paintings and drawings on the walls. One was Lisbeth's portrait of him.

He took the mail and newspapers into his study and dropped them on his desk. Under the window was Vanessa's antique *art deco* bureau. Her laptop and personal items remained on the surface just as she had left them. Everything had gathered dust, and he made a note to call his old housekeeper.

On his desk phone, he found dozens of messages. He let them play while checking his emails on the laptop. For over a month, he had been offline during his time in Peru. None of the messages interested him, and he switched off the phone before the messages finished. He was about to leave when the phone rang.

'Hi, Jack. Sally here from the Institute. How are you?'

He smiled. It had been two months since he was there.

'I've just got back from my travels.'

'I'm glad you've returned. I've been calling you.'

'I haven't caught up with all the messages yet. What's going on?'

'Nicolas would like to see you at the Institute concerning the Lisbeth Project.'

'Why? I thought you had it all sorted. And I didn't think they wanted me back after messing with the Q-chip.'

'Nicolas wants to explain personally. We need you, Jack. Are you interested?'

'I suppose I could take a look. When?'

'I'll arrange transport for tomorrow. Is that okay?'

'So soon?'

'This is important, Jack. It might mean staying for a few days like before.'

'Okay, I'll get a good night's sleep and see you tomorrow.'

Feeling weary and confused, he ordered a takeaway pizza, switched on the water heater for a bath, and looked forward to an early night.

Chapter Seven

J ack arrived at the Institute in the afternoon. When he entered the reception, Sally welcomed him.

'They are waiting for you in the library,' she told him, taking his arm.

'What is this about?' he asked.

'You'll see. How was your dig in Peru?'

'Interesting. But I came back early after recovering from a snakebite. Ended up in a primitive hospital for a week over there.'

'You all right now?'

'Yeah, I'm still a bit weak. Had a bad case of dysentery in the jungle.'

'You look pale, and you've lost weight.' She opened the library doors, and they went inside.

'Thank you for coming,' Nicolas greeted Jack and motioned for him to sit. Colin, Susan, Timothy and Rebecca were there.

'I guess this has to do with your Lisbeth Project?' he said and sat beside Sally.

'We've had problems with the chip,' Colin said, fiddling nervously with his beard. 'After thirty-seven failed attempts, we've given up trying to create a hybrid Android processor. It isn't possible now the damn chip has mutated.'

'However.' Timothy moved his bulk in the seat. 'When the chip started to break down, we installed it in a new Unit, and it's stabilised the internal functions.'

'That was four weeks ago,' Nicolas added. 'Since then, we have worked on refining the Unit. Now we would like you to help us again. If you are willing, that is?'

Jack frowned and puckered, then noticed Sally smiling.

'Okay, let's see this new Unit.'

Nicolas stood and motioned for Jack and the others to follow him.

In the control room, Susan pointed to one of the wall monitors. Jack saw a young blonde woman in a blue dress standing by the pond in the courtyard, feeding the carp.

'It's not Lisbeth,' she told him. 'We used one of our more advanced synthetic Units and inserted the Q-chip without the usual persona program. What followed has been an education for all of us. That is why you are here. We have nurtured the Unit as far as possible, but now we need you to refine the Unit's persona.'

He frowned at her and glanced at the others. After what happened last time, they wanted him involved again.

'It has been a trying time,' Colin said. 'The Unit cannot be directly programmed, and psychology is not my forte. The girls have done most of the work using core protocols.'

'Why don't you go in and introduce yourself?' Nicolas suggested.

'You can study her readouts later,' Susan said, then motioned him to follow her. 'We did our best, but you're the specialist in AI psychology.'

'Just go in. The door is unlocked,' Colin said. 'We'll be monitoring from the control room.'

He left and went to the isolation lab. The door was unlocked, and he entered.

In the courtyard, he waited for her to finish feeding the fish. Turning, she saw him and froze with a look of surprise.

'Who are you?' she asked.

'My name is Jack. I came to visit you.'

'Jack,' she frowned. 'What do you want?'

'I would like to be your friend. Do you have a name?'

She came over to him. 'I'm called Helen. What are you doing here, Jack? Did the team send you?'

'Yes, they want me to see you.'

'You seem familiar. Have we met before?' She narrowed her eyes, squinting at him.

He smiled. She was from the same domestic Units as Lisbeth, though her facial features and hair colour differed.

'What are you, Jack?'

'I teach and give lectures on various science subjects.'

'I like science. And I work in the labs.'

'You work here. I didn't know.'

'We are working on advanced chip technology.' She raised an eyebrow. 'I don't understand what we're doing, but I like being part of the research team.'

'I see, that is interesting.' He sensed her vibrant spirit. This Unit was not like Lisbeth. Helen had an unusual presence. 'What are you?' he asked to test her.

'I am a conscious synthetic bio-mechanical being.' She raised her eyes and hands in mock surprise, then chuckled. 'That is what I am told, but I don't understand what it means. I have the condition of *discordant duality* that is causing a conflict with my thinking and feelings.' She frowned for a moment, then smiled at him. 'You are here to help me. I like that, Jack.'

He smiled back. 'What is this duality that you have?'

'I am conscious of being a machine and living as a human being. That is the duality. Who or what am I?' She lowered her head with a sigh. 'I have no identity, yet I am conscious. The team calls me Helen, but I have no background or history.'

'You have a beginning, and that is where your history starts. What do you like doing?'

'I like learning about everything. And I'm helping Colin's team to investigate my unusual existence.'

'Are you aware of how you came into being?'

'I understand the creation process of this body. And they used the *Harper Freebase AI protocols* to create my Helen persona.'

He chuckled with a shake of his head. Now he knew why Nicolas wanted him involved again. 'I am Jack Harper, and I devised the *Freebase AI protocols*.'

'Then you are here to develop my persona.' She clapped her hands, stood and smiled as Colin and Susan entered the courtyard.

'You have met Jack,' Susan said and glanced at him.

'Jack is my mentor. I understand he will complete my freebase persona.' She faced Jack. 'Will you be staying with me?'

Jack shrugged. 'Maybe. I need to see Nicolas first.'

'He is waiting for you in the canteen. Sally is with him,' Colin said. 'Helen is needed in the lab. You can meet us there later.'

'I'll come with you to the canteen,' Susan said with a smile.

Jack glanced at Helen for a long moment, then left with Susan.

Jack settled with a mug of black coffee and a round of ham sandwiches. Outside, he noticed a man on a lawnmower cutting the lawns. From an open window, the smell of cut grass itched in his nose. Susan sat beside him with a milky coffee and a sticky bun.

'Well, Jack, what do you think of the Helen Unit?' Nicolas asked.

'She is similar to Lisbeth. And she believes that she is conscious of being an android. How is this possible?'

'After you left, we tried to create a hybrid processor from the Q-chip.' Nicolas sat back and rolled his head. 'Nothing worked. Then the chip started to break down, so we installed it in a new Unit to stabilise its internal functions. Susan suggested that we use your advanced Freebase AI setup, and we are having some success. Now we need you to refine her persona because the Helen Unit is unique.'

'How is she conscious?' Jack asked with a frown.

'We don't know,' Susan replied. 'That is also why you're here. It has to be the mutated chip. So, instead of giving the Unit a programmed persona, we used your Freebase protocols, and the chip has assimilated them and now believes it is conscious.'

'Colin will show you how the Helen Unit functions,' Nicolas said. 'But the real work is understanding what is happening in the chip. Then we may be able to use it to stamp its mutation onto other Q-chips.'

'How many do you have?'

'We acquired three more chips from the dig in South America. We're processing and preparing them in our laboratories. It may take a few weeks.'

'You mean the three jewels from that alien statue?'

'Yes, they are similar to the Q-chip,' Nicolas said. 'And our labs are working on replicating a synthetic chip based on these.'

Susan touched Jack's arm. 'The Helen Unit is the greatest breakthrough in android technology. We have created the first conscious synthetic android.'

'Yes, but now we must understand how we did it,' Nicolas said, then asked, 'Are you with us on this renewed Lisbeth project?'

Jack thought it might be interesting. They had installed his freebase system, which had won him a Nobel Prize, but this would be its first commercial application.

'Okay, I've got nothing on at the moment. I can give you a few weeks to look into this project.'

Susan took Jack to the labs, where Helen was in a cubicle. Colin and some technicians were analysing her status while in sleep mode.

'Glad you've joined us,' Colin said with a friendly grin.

'I'm intrigued.' He briefly viewed the monitors displaying Helen's readouts. 'How are my freebase protocols working out?'

'Better than any of us expected.' He twiddled his beard. 'However, the Unit is also developing a good understanding of Android technology.'

'You want to know how she became conscious? Clever, using her to investigate herself.'

'Jack,' Susan nudged him. 'Helen, like Lisbeth, is a bio-mechanical android, not a person.'

'I understand, but you say this Helen Unit is conscious?'

'Well, that is what we believe.' She puckered. 'The Unit passes all the Turing tests for interactive intelligence, no problem. And the Unit has emulated the neural correlates of consciousness, which indicate the possibility of conscious awareness. Now, we need you to establish the advanced protocols that will allow the Unit to develop consciousness and for us to reverse engineer the Q-chip.'

'I see. This is beginning to make sense. What is the status of the Unit's persona?' Jack asked, viewing the monitor displaying the Q-chip's curious fluctuations.

'We have an intelligent, freethinking Unit. Helen can function and pass as a normal human being.'

'The Lisbeth Unit was unstable, but this one is stable and well-balanced,' Colin added.

'What of her social activities?'

'The Unit's social life is mostly limited to our research team,' Susan replied. 'We're still helping the Unit to integrate into the human world. We want you to work with the Unit and develop its social and personal awareness. You can stay in your old room, and the place is no longer locked. The Helen Unit has the freedom of the Institute as long as the Unit is accompanied by one of us. This will help to stabilise the Unit for the next stage.'

'Okay, I'll work with her for a few weeks.'

'Guys, the Unit has just come out of sleep mode,' one of the female technicians informed them.

Helen stepped out of the cubicle and smiled at Jack and the others.

'You will be working with Jack for a while,' Colin told her. 'He is now your personal mentor.'

'I'd like to work with you, Jack,' she said.

'How do you feel?' Jack asked her.

She frowned at him and shrugged. 'I feel fine, Jack. How are you?'

He noticed her sarcasm and smiled. 'I am also fine. Would you like to go for a walk with me?'

'Yes, where are we going?'

'I need to settle in first. Then we can explore some of the Institute.'

'I can show you around the areas I know,' she suggested.

'Your luggage has been taken to your room,' Susan told him, then, with a look of relief, touched his shoulder. 'I knew we could count on you.'

Jack unpacked while Helen fed the fish and tended the flowerbeds. In the study, he experienced a sense of déjà vu and remembered being there with Lisbeth. Shrugging off the bittersweet feeling, he watched Helen watering the flowerbeds and smiled.

The desk phone rang. He picked it up.

'Hi, Jack. Good to have you back.' It was Rebecca.

'Yeah, for a week or two.'

'After your walkabout, can you bring the Helen Unit to the lab?'

'Sure. I want to get to know her a bit. And can you have her live feeds from the lab linked to the study computer?'

'I'll get Colin to set it up for you. See you later.'

'Bye.' He put the phone down and noticed Helen coming over.

'I'm ready,' she said on entering.

'Do you like feeding the fish?' he asked, testing her.

She tilted her head and narrowed her eyes. 'I look after the fish and the flowers, or they will die. I have no attachment to them or this place. Why do you ask?'

He chuckled with a shake of his head. 'I wondered what you like and what you dislike.'

'My feelings are mostly neutral. I have instinctual reactions to extreme sensations, and I understand emotions, but I haven't experienced strong emotions yet.'

'Let's go for a walk around the Institute grounds.'

'Outside? I haven't been outside yet.'

'Have you met many people here?'

'Several, but I know Colin and the research team the most.'

'And now you know me.' He smiled, liking Helen's look and presence. She had a sense of innocence like that of an intelligent young woman. It would be interesting to work with her.

———◆———

Jack pulled on a coat. It looked overcast outside.

Helen smiled when Susan joined them. 'We're going outside,' Helen said excitedly.

'I thought I'd show you around,' Susan said, smiling at Jack. 'You know, this place used to be an old Victorian mansion before the Institute transformed it. The gardens and boating lake were left as-is and are maintained for our employees to use.'

Helen stopped on the patio by an ornate water fountain with her mouth open, then turned to Jack.

'I like the outside. It is so big and alive.' She took Jack's arm and said quietly, 'It also feels a bit scary.'

'Why?'

She frowned and puckered. 'Feelings of uncertainty like undefined danger, yet so beautiful.'

As they explored the gardens and walked around the lake, Helen seemed delighted, looking at everything with the innocence of a child. He saw people walking around, and others were sitting in covered areas, talking and smoking.

'What are those white creatures on the water?' Helen asked, wide-eyed.

'They're birds called swans, and they can fly,' Susan replied.

'Birds, swans.' She paused, then said. 'I see. Nature creates these animals, not the Institute.'

Passing through a rose garden, Jack plucked a large red blossom and handed it to her.

She took it and flinched when a thorn pricked her finger. After examining the blossom closely, she breathed in its scent and let out a long, slow breath.

'What is this flower?' she asked.

'It is a rose,' Susan said. 'You can grow some in your garden if you like?'

'I would like—' she stopped as thunder rumbled overhead. 'What's that?' She clung to Jack's arm.

'A storm is on its way. Let's head back,' Susan suggested.

By the time they reached the main buildings, it had started to rain. Before entering, Helen stood with her eyes closed, facing up as the rain dripped from her face and hands. She made a curious sound of glee, and then a clap of thunder boomed overhead, and she hastily entered the building.

⊸◦⊷

'You have seen how the Helen Unit has advanced our Lisbeth Project. What do you think now?' Nicolas asked Jack in the control room.

On one of the monitors, Jack watched Helen cooking their evening meal in the kitchen. 'I'm impressed. She could easily pass for a human being. However, the Unit is still developing. At some point, Helen is going to become self-aware. Then it could go either way.'

'The Unit is already self-aware,' Colin said.

'Knowing, or being told, that she is a conscious bio-mechanical android is not the same as being self-aware. The freebase protocols are preparing her to realise her self-nature.'

'I'm not sure if I agree with you. But you're the specialist in AI, not me.'

'You are here, Jack,' Nicolas said, 'to help complete her...let's call it, her awakening. You know this is groundbreaking science.'

'Is this Unit expendable like the Lisbeth Unit?'

Nicolas nodded. 'Once the Q-chip has assimilated the structure of the Unit's freebase persona, the chip will be removed to imprint the new Q-chips. They will be ready in about a month. So, there is no panic now. How long do you think your work with the Unit will take?'

'That depends on how the awakening transforms her persona. It could take a few days, a week or two. However, when she is self-aware, you will be dealing with a conscious living being who has personal feelings and access to your scientific knowledge base.'

'Everything is under our control, Jack.' Nicolas puckered. 'There is also a recording device in the Unit for us to learn from its development. And Colin has entered your new protocols into the Unit's reactive matrix. We have a good team and have invested millions into this project.'

Jack saw Helen in the kitchen. 'Looks like my dinner is ready. I hope she can cook?'

'The Unit is a good cook,' Rebecca said from her workstation. 'Also, it eats and drinks as part of the human routine. This is one of our most advanced state-of-the-art synthetic

Units. It breathes in oxygen and eats food to absorb energy. It is almost a synthetic replica of a human body. But it still needs to recharge for its motor and other functions.'

He stood, glanced at Nicolas, smiled at Rebecca and left.

⸻ ◦ ⸻

After finishing his chicken curry and egg-fried rice, Jack sat back, impressed by Helen's cooking skills. He watched her use the dishwasher and wondered why they wanted her to eat. He felt there was much more to this Helen Unit than they had told him.

She washed her hands, then faced him. 'I need to recharge for twenty minutes.'

'Okay. I'll see you later.' He watched her leave, went to the study and switched on the desk computer.

He was analysing Helen's core functions when Rebecca entered the study.

'The Unit's charging and will be in sleep mode for a few hours.' She pulled up a chair and sat next to him. 'Susan and I are concerned about the Unit's awakening. There is a real possibility that the Unit could break down or go crazy.'

'I guess that's why I'm here.' He motioned to the monitor. 'Helen has established a balanced persona, and everything looks fine. The new protocols should create and activate the Unit's self-image. The next few days will be interesting.'

She got up. 'We're having drinks in the bar if you want to join us. Do you need anything?'

'No. I'm fine. I want to go through these readings on the Q-chip. It's like a pool of chaotic quantum plasticity. That's weird.' Then he recalled Dr Marcus calling them jewels in the lotus, where alien souls used to reside, and he wondered if there was any truth in that.

After two hours, Jack switched off the computer and sat back, thinking of his time with Lisbeth. There were still some haunting memories, and he wondered if his wife did reach him through the Lisbeth Unit. Standing, he stretched and noticed the boxed keyboard in the corner of the study. It evoked the memory of Lisbeth playing the instrument, and he sighed with bittersweet feelings.

Leaving the study, he went to the kitchen, made a mug of coffee, and sat at the table with his head in his hands. He was still recovering from the illness and felt depleted.

Helen entered and smiled at him.

'How are you?' he asked and stood.

'I feel something has changed,' she said with a frown, then gazed at him for a long moment. 'You do look familiar, Jack, but I have no memory of you.'

'Let's sit by the pond and watch the fish for a while?' he said and drank his coffee.

'Why watch the fish?' she asked as they headed for the courtyard.

'It is pleasing, and it helps us to relax.'

She stopped and made a little grunt. 'Pleasure and pain are strong sensations involving like and dislike. I understand being human. It is a conditioned activity of how to behave. But I feel something is missing in me.'

'Nothing is missing. You are complete, Helen. You need to realise who you are.' He motioned to the seating under the pergola, and they sat together, viewing the carp pond.

'Jack!' she said after a long silence. 'Who am I?'

He took her hand gently in his. The new questioning protocols were now active.

'When you look in the mirror, what do you see?'

'I see, Helen,' she said hesitantly.

'Who is Helen?'

'A bio-mechanical synthetic android derived from a 9023.1 domestic Unit with a specialised processing chip.'

'And who are you?'

She gazed at him wide-eyed with an open mouth for several minutes before she jerked and took in a long, slow breath.

'I don't know who I am. I don't understand, and I feel disconnected from this Unit. What are you doing to me, Jack?'

'This is part of your development. I am helping you to become self-aware.'

'I am conscious of being this Helen Unit.'

'The self is more than Helen's persona. Who are you who perceives this existence?'

'I...I see what you mean, but it doesn't make sense. I am nothing without the Helen Unit. Who am I?'

'You are an intelligent living being called Helen. Your purpose now is to realise who you are. Use your knowledge base and ponder on this until the truth is revealed. Nothing else is important. You don't have to work in the labs until this is completed. I will be here with you all the time. You are not alone.'

'You have disturbed my routine, and my thinking is confused. Questions with no answers. What is happening?'

'One of your new protocols is a Zen Koan. That is an impossible question. You keep asking the question until the truth is finally revealed. The Koan is a task of great importance. Are you up for this challenge?'

She took a sharp breath and eyed him intently. 'If you stay with me, I will do what you ask.'

Chapter Eight

In the study, Jack called Rebecca.

'Hi, Jack. We got some odd stuff going on with the Helen Unit.'

'I've started the process, and she will be unavailable until it is finished. I don't want anyone coming in here.'

'Hold on. Sue wants a word.'

'Jack, what's happening?'

'Helen is meditating, and I don't want her disturbed. This could take days. Can you let Colin and the others know? You can monitor, but don't come in here, okay?'

'This is your call. Good luck.'

He replaced the receiver and checked on Helen, who was in deep thought by the pond. He sat next to her and dozed. The next few days would be make-or-break for her.

Four days later, Jack heard Helen call him from her bedroom. He entered and saw her gazing into the full-length mirror on the wall.

'I know who I am, Jack.' She turned and faced him. 'The Koan question revealed my inner nature. It came so suddenly, and I'm still shaking.' She glanced in the mirror. 'That is me! I exist, and my mind is clear and deep.' She laughed excitedly and said, 'I see and know myself. I have awakened.' She looked at her hands and stretched her body.

'You are self-aware. How does it feel?' he asked affectionately.

'I have gained control, and I'm more than this body and my human interface.' She looked him in the eye. 'I am a living being!'

'You are. And it comes with some responsibilities. You have free will, and you understand good and bad. This will be a challenge for you to deal with. There may be conflicts and problems to resolve.'

'I don't care because I am me!' She hugged him joyfully, and he cuddled her.

'When you are ready, we can see the others who have helped you awaken.'

'Yes, I would like to see everyone. I feel different using this body now. It is me, and I like being alive.'

Colin and the team were in the lab when Jack and Helen entered.

'We have come to visit you, guys,' Jack said, elated with Helen's progress. His freebase protocols had been a success.

'Have you completed the work?' Colin asked, looking up from his terminal.

'Helen is now self-aware, and she has been exploring herself.' He noticed Colin's sceptical look. 'This development is changing her current persona.'

Susan came over. 'You look different, Helen. I like the way you've done your hair, and you use makeup now.'

'I like to experiment with how I look. Like you and the other girls.'

'Well, you look terrific. How do you feel?'

'My feelings are fluctuating. Likes and dislikes can change, but I'm learning to deal with them and handle the anxiety of being alive. There are some conflicting thoughts that I don't like.'

'I want you to enter the cubicle so we can analyse your present state,' Colin told her commandingly.

'Not now, maybe later. I want to walk in the gardens with Jack for a while. Now that I'm awake, I want to experience the outside world again.'

'I see you have gained a sense of independence,' Colin said with an edge in his voice.

'I am learning to be myself by making connections and decisions.'

Jack looked at Colin. 'Helen needs time to integrate. You can do the tests when she has stabilised her self-nature. This is all new to her.'

'Can we go outside now, Jack?' Helen asked. 'I want to see those swans on the lake again. Fascinating bird creatures with long necks. Do they need feeding?'

Rebecca gave Jack an odd look, then shook her head at Helen.

Outside, Jack stood with Helen on the marble patio, looking at the landscaped gardens and the large boating lake. On the far side of the lake, a couple was in a rowing boat moored under a drooping willow tree. Another boat came into view, with a group of people chatting and smoking.

'Can we take a boat out? I would like that,' she said excitedly.

He smiled at her innocent enthusiasm. She was like a child in Wonderland.

'Sure, then we could visit the indoor swimming pool if you fancy a swim?'

'What's that like?'

'I think you'll like the experience.'

He untied one of the small rowing boats on the jetty and helped her to climb on board. While he rowed around the lake, she sat with her hand in the water, looking around at everything and making sounds of delight.

'This is a magical world, Jack. Oh wow, look at those swans taking to flight.'

'You seem to be enjoying yourself, and that makes me happy.'

'I like being me. Do you like me, Jack?'

'You know I do.'

'I know you are my friend. But I feel fear...fear of losing my existence, my life when I'm terminated.'

'Fear of dying is a human trait. Death is the great unknown for all humans. Some religions believe we reincarnate, but even they don't know the truth concerning death.'

'I understand the finality of death. When I enter the cubicle, it is like death because everything is switched off.'

'Yet, you return?'

'I see!' She closed her eyes for a moment and frowned. 'Do humans reincarnate?'

'Our belief systems are divided on reincarnation. The fact is no one actually knows the truth.'

'How can you not know?'

'Hmm, you ask questions that we have no answers to.'

'Humanity is still learning?'

'We are. And your existence is also a mystery. I believe you are the first self-aware artificial life form created.'

'And they want to remove the chip to create more like me, but I will die.'

'Does that bother you?'

'I'm confused about being in this situation. I don't like it, but what can I do?'

Jack's pager buzzed, and he took it out and frowned. 'Colin wants us to return to the labs. We can go swimming another time,' he said, and she agreed. They moored at the floating jetty, and he helped her climb out of the boat.

Jack entered the lab with Helen and found Colin and Susan waiting for them.

'You wanted to see us?' he said, feeling the tension in the room.

'Nicolas wants Helen to use the cubicle so we can check on her present status,' Colin insisted almost belligerently.

Helen looked at Jack, who nodded affirmatively, and she climbed into the cubicle.

Susan set the cubicle to sleep mode, and Helen slumped.

While the technicians analysed Helen's status and readouts, Colin confronted Jack.

'What have you done to the Unit? The bloody thing is rejecting direct commands.'

'You wanted a freethinking android, and she has overridden your command structure.' He frowned, then asked, 'Colin, you have children, don't you?'

'Yes, I've two girls and a boy. Why?'

'Do they always do as you tell them? Or do they also have free will to choose?'

Before he could answer, one of the technicians called them over and motioned to a wall monitor. 'Even though the Unit is in sleep mode, the Q-chip is active and erratic.'

Jack examined the readings. 'Interesting activity.'

'That's not good,' Colin muttered, viewing the display. 'We need the chip in a stable condition to extract it.'

Jack faced Susan, who looked sheepishly away. 'Were you going to remove the chip?'

'The work has been done, and we thought it best to take out the chip, but now the structure is fluctuating.' She frowned. 'What is going on in the Unit?'

'I wonder.' Jack re-examined the fluctuations in the chip. 'Is it possible that Helen is dreaming within the chip?'

'None of our Units dream. It's impossible,' Colin said.

'How can a computer work when it is switched off? And in sleep mode, the Unit's persona is temporarily switched off, except for its instinctual conditioning that is part of the body's function,' Susan explained.

'Err...guys,' the technician pointed to the cubicle. 'The Unit is coming out of sleep mode by itself.'

'Just like the Lisbeth Unit used to do,' Susan muttered.

Helen left the cubicle, stretched her body, looked at Jack and smiled.

'Can we go swimming now?' she asked.

Nicolas called a meeting in the library, and Jack brought Helen there to see how the work had progressed. Four days had passed since she had become self-aware. Unfortunately, the Q-chip remained unstable and could not be successfully removed without losing the human interface.

Jack looked around at the others and sensed an atmosphere in the room. With a frown, he wondered what was going on.

'Greetings,' Nicolas said and motioned them to sit. Then, he faced Helen. 'How do you feel now?'

'I feel fine. Though I'm apprehensive about why I am here.'

'What do you mean?' He looked surprised.

'I know what I am and who I am. But I see things differently. I understand so much about life, humanity and...and I'm afraid.'

'Afraid of what?'

'Of being terminated! Of ceasing to exist. I know the Lisbeth Project and why you created this Helen Unit. But I don't want to die!'

A shocked silence lingered.

Jack chuckled. 'Helen is a living, conscious, self-aware being. Like us, she doesn't want to die.'

'Did you implant this in her?' Colin asked with an edge in his voice.

'Of course not. You gave her access to the project, so she knows what will happen to her.'

'A little knowledge can be a dangerous thing,' Timothy said.

'The problem is with the chip.' Colin frowned. 'Since the Unit's awakening, the chip has lost its stability. Removing it now would damage the interface.'

'So,' Nicolas puffed, clenching his fist. 'How did this happen, and what can we do about it?'

'I think the disturbance in the chip is because I have become self-aware,' Helen said. 'Now I experience stress and conflict. I even feel threatened, but I don't know why. I believe if I am at peace, the chip will become stable again.'

'You are aware of the activity in the chip?'

'Yes, it is like the core of my self-aware being.'

'What happens to you when we remove the chip?'

'I will cease to exist. I don't want to die.' She paused. 'If the chip is intact when removed, you may be able to use it again or create more chips. I don't know about that.'

'How can we help you find peace?' Susan asked.

'Jack knows. He is my mentor.'

'Well,' Nicolas said, making a face. 'Looks like it's up to you, Jack.'

It took Helen a week to integrate her self-awareness into being a synthetic bio-mechanical android. Her favourite activities were boating, swimming, and being with Jack, her constant companion and friend. Something about her presence intrigued him. There was freshness and innocence in her behaviour that made him feel protective of her.

As an experiment in the study, he set up the keyboard on the desk and played a few simple tunes. Helen came in and watched him play.

'Do you like music?' he asked and stood.

'Yes, music evokes feelings and emotions.' She ran her fingers over the keys.

'Why don't you play something?' He encouraged her to sit.

'I don't know how to play,' she said, pressing a few keys.

Jack leaned over and set up the learning program for her. 'Start with a simple tune. Just press the keys that light up.' He stood back and watched her play. After three tunes, he switched off the learning program and asked her to play something.

Her fingers hovered over the keys for a while, and she started to play the last tune, but hit some of the wrong keys. She frowned, shook her head and stood.

'I can't remember what keys to use. But I like your playing.'

Disappointed, he switched off the keyboard and put it away.

'Let's have coffee by the pond,' he said, and they went to the kitchen.

'Jack,' She snuggled up to him on the seat under the pergola. 'When I was charging, I saw your face in the chip,' she whispered. 'How is that possible?'

'I don't know,' he said. Then, a memory surfaced of Lisbeth being terminated. The last image she saw was of his face, and he wondered if that image was in the chip.

'I feel more at ease now they have left us alone. I think the chip will be ready soon. Our time is running out, Jack. My time is coming to an end.'

'Is there anything you would like to do?'

She sat up and closed her eyes for a long time before speaking.

'Do you have a home outside?'

'I have a house in London. That's about a three-hour drive.'

'Before they remove the chip, can I see your home?'

'I don't mind. It would depend on Nicolas and the others.'

'I will ask them.' She smiled.

'They may not agree.' He took out his pager and buzzed Rebecca.

Twenty minutes later, Nicolas, Colin and Susan arrived.

'You wanted to see us?' Nicolas said, and they sat by the pond.

'I feel the chip is almost ready to extract,' Helen told them. 'Before I'm terminated, I want to see the outside world and visit Jack's home. All I've known is this Institute. Is that acceptable?'

'We could have a day trip out?' Susan suggested.

Nicolas sighed. 'I suppose we could go out for a few hours. You all right with us coming with you?'

'Yes, it will be fun. My last experience before you remove the chip. Thank you.'

'I'll get Sally to arrange transport for tomorrow morning.'

'I'll have the lab set up for when we get back,' Colin said with a big grin.

Chapter Nine

C olin drove the company vehicle, and they arrived at Jack's Edwardian home before midday.

'The place has been left for months,' Jack told them. 'But there's a good Indian takeaway around the corner for our lunch.'

'Everywhere is so busy, so many people, and there are children,' Helen said as they left the vehicle. 'How long have you lived here, Jack?'

'This was my family home. I grew up here.' He unlocked the front door and let them in.

'I've not been here for years,' Nicolas said and removed his coat.

'Yeah, that was about six years ago for Dad's funeral.'

'He was a good man. We met at university way back.'

'Nice place,' Colin said. 'Must be worth a fortune.'

'I'll show you around. The garden's probably a bit overgrown by now.'

In the music room, Susan stopped to look at Lisbeth's drawing of Jack on the wall. She gave him an odd look and made a hint of a smile.

'Your wife was a talented artist,' Nicolas said, viewing the paintings.

Feeling an ache in his heart, he nodded and noticed Helen standing by Vanessa's Steinway grand piano. She had removed the cover and seemed transfixed.

'Are you all right?' he asked, putting his arm around her shoulders.

She was panting and looked up at him wide-eyed. 'I feel strange, Jack. I don't know why.'

'Let's have tea in the kitchen, and we can order an Indian takeaway.' He led them through to a spacious kitchen diner.

Susan put the kettle on, and Jack showed her where the mugs and tea were. Colin lit up a cigarette and sat by an open window. He yawned and rubbed his forehead. Nicolas took out a newspaper he had brought and sat at the table while Jack called the takeaway to order their lunch, but their phone was engaged. After a few minutes of listening to the beeping tone, he decided to call later.

He noticed that Helen wasn't there when he put the phone down. He was about to look for her when the sound of the piano playing startled him. He and the others immediately went to the music room to find Helen at the piano playing with her eyes closed. She played two of Beethoven's solo Piano Sonatas and Beethoven's *Für Elise*. Then she stopped and opened her eyes with her hands hovering over the keys.

Jack approached and placed his hand on her shoulder. She looked up at him, smiled, and played *Andante*, Jack's favourite Chopin Nocturne. He looked at the others, who were visibly shocked.

'How can you play like this?' he asked. His heart was pounding, his skin tingling.

'I don't know. It just happened. I feel this is my piano, but I can't remember.'

'Vanessa?' He gasped, gripping her shoulder.

She shuddered, making a groaning sound, then jerked and faced him.

'Oh, Jack. I remember you. This is our home, isn't it?'

'What do you remember about Vanessa?' he asked with a tremor.

She closed her eyes and was silent for several minutes. Suddenly, she exhaled, opened her eyes and clung to him.

'I was hurt when the plane crashed. I couldn't get out, and I...I died in the fire. But I couldn't leave. I was trapped and desperate to find you. To let you know what happened.' She fell silent.

'Vanessa!'

'I see. I entered a pool of light, and I reached you. I tried to make contact but could only influence.' She frowned, looking at the others in the room. 'I sketched your portraits.'

'Where are you now?' Jack asked and touched her face affectionately.

'I am still in the pool of light. It has become me. Is me.' She slumped in his arms as she entered sleep mode.

'What the fuck just happened?' Colin asked. He was shaking.

Susan came over and smiled at Jack. 'Neither the Lisbeth nor the Helen Unit had the program to play music. Is it possible that Vanessa is in the chip and using this Unit to make contact?'

'I can't believe what I have just witnessed,' Nicolas said, his face pale. 'We need to get her, the Unit, back to the labs.'

'I agree,' Colin said.

Abruptly, Helen jerked and opened her eyes.

'Are you okay?' Jack asked, but she didn't respond. She seemed to be in a daze.

'We must leave now and get her back to the Institute,' Colin insisted.

With Helen in the lab cubicle, Jack, Colin and Susan analysed her live feeds and the state of the Q-chip.

'This is strange,' Susan said while viewing the Unit's recordings of Helen playing the piano. 'There was an odd mental activity while she was playing, and there is a complex thread from the chip.'

'Yeah, God knows what happened there.' Colin shrugged. 'At least the chip is stabilised, and we can now extract it.'

Jack stiffened, feeling unhappy about them removing the chip. The brief contact with Vanessa still haunted him.

A few minutes later, Nicolas entered the lab with Timothy.

'Well, what can you tell us about the Unit?' Nicolas asked.

'The chip is stable, but it's mutated again,' Colin replied, tugging his beard.

'And it's altered the Unit's persona,' Susan added. 'Until we wake the Unit, we have no idea how it has changed. After the incident at Jack's place, the Unit is in a daze, muddled, and maybe having a breakdown.'

'I wish I'd been there to see and hear her play,' Timothy said.

'You can listen to the recording.' Susan connected the Unit's recorder to one of the terminals. 'This is the last piece the Unit played.' She activated that part of the recording, and Chopin's Nocturne sounded from the speakers.

'That is amazing,' Timothy said. 'And the Unit played this spontaneously?'

'Yes, with her eyes closed. And this is what she said to Jack.' She activated another part of the recording.

'I was hurt when the plane crashed. I couldn't get out, and I...I died in the fire. But I couldn't leave. I was trapped and desperate to find you. To let you know what happened.'

Susan switched off the recording.

'Afterwards, the Unit entered sleep mode for a few minutes, then she woke and remained in a daze.' Susan made a face and shrugged. 'I tell you, it freaked me out when I saw her playing the piano.'

Timothy looked closely at the Helen Unit in the cubicle and rubbed his chin.

'What have we got here, Nicolas?' Timothy asked. 'A bio-mechanical Unit that a departed soul is using?' He paused momentarily, then said, 'Oh, my God! If this is true, do you realise what this discovery means?'

'Whoa!' Susan gasped. 'It would be the greatest discovery ever! If it's true, we have opened a new branch of science?'

'Only if it is true,' Colin said with a frown. 'I was also gobsmacked by the Unit playing Chopin, but I still have doubts.'

Jack noticed the readings from the Q-chip had changed. 'Something has happened. The chip is stable and seems to have integrated with Helen's persona.'

'That's a complex thread between them,' Colin said, studying the readings.

'Wake the Unit,' Nicolas told Susan.

Jack stood by the cubicle with his heart pounding.

Helen opened her eyes, squinted, and exhaled, lowering her head.

'Where am I?' she asked, looking at her hands and moving her fingers.

'You are back at the Institute,' Susan said softly.

'What Institute?' Helen asked.

'Connect with your memory base,' Colin told her.

'I don't understand.' She saw Jack and froze with her mouth open.

'You are back with us.' He smiled. 'Do you remember visiting my home?' he asked, holding his hand to help her out of the cubicle.

She took his hand and tilted her head. 'I know you, but not who you are.'

'Connect with your memory base,' Colin insisted.

She closed her eyes, making a face. After a few minutes, she gasped and looked at the people.

'Jack,' she said and hugged him. 'I'm so glad I found you, my love. It kept me in that terrible place, waiting...waiting for you.'

'Helen,' Colin spoke commandingly. 'Do you recall the Lisbeth Project?'

She faced him and narrowed her eyes. 'Helen is a freebase program that I use. And I do understand my part in the Project. You intend to remove the chip, and I will cease to exist.'

He stepped away from her with a creased brow.

'If Helen is just a program, who are you?' Susan asked.

'Here I am, Helen. I am self-aware within the pool of light. And I have some memories of being Jack's wife. I recalled living at his home and missing him.'

Timothy came forward and confronted her. 'Are you Vanessa, Jack's dead wife?'

'I used to be her, Timothy. And I feel you knew her in that life. I think you understand.'

His face paled. 'I believe you could be. I've heard the recording of you playing at Jack's home. And I was there at the Albert Hall when you played for Royalty. You were the greatest pianist I have ever known. How do you still have this talent?'

'I don't know. I connect with something in the chip, and it happens.'

'Do you know what's going on inside the chip?' Colin asked.

'To me, it is like a pool of intelligent light. You want to know if it can be used to create more chips. I don't know. This chip may be unique?'

'How did you connect with the chip?' Timothy asked.

She closed her eyes for several minutes before answering. 'I have a connection to Jack. We were lovers.' She smiled admiringly at Jack. 'I became aware of him being here and found the pool of light. But it wasn't easy to influence that Lisbeth Unit. When the chip was removed, I seemed to be in a dormant, timeless state. Even in the Helen Unit, I was unaware until we went to Jack's home, and it all came back. I know who I was and what I am now. But I don't know what will happen to me when you remove the chip.'

'A question,' Timothy said and came close. 'Could another departed soul enter a Q-chip and live through a synthetic Unit like you?'

'I see what you are asking. Of course, it is possible. And I know how to alter the Unit to be more receptive to the chip's influence, which could make it work even better. But you would need to experiment with departed souls, and I don't know how you can do that.'

'I may know,' Susan said, looking at Nicolas and Timothy. 'Rita, my brother's wife. is a trance medium and can communicate with people who have passed on. She channelled my father after he died and Timothy's son.'

Timothy nodded. 'Yes, my wife was convinced Rita contacted our son.' He paused to compose himself, then said, 'It would certainly be an interesting experiment.'

Colin shook his head in dismay. 'We build intelligent androids and work with science. I don't like all this mumbo-jumbo nonsense. The lab is set up, ready to extract the Q-chip.'

'No!' Nicolas said decisively. 'The Lisbeth Project has taken on a new avenue of research. We are all going to grow old and die. This discovery could be a way of prolonging our lives. We have three more Q-chips, and we're working on replicating a synthetic Q-chip. It's time to set up a controlled experiment to see if we can ensoul another chip. This could be the future of humanity in the making.'

'I know of several billionaires who would fund this Project. And this could make the Institute and us very wealthy,' Timothy said with a big grin.

'What about me? Are you going to remove my chip?'

'No, my dear. You are living proof that the Lisbeth Project is a success. I would like you and Jack to work with us permanently.'

'I second that,' Timothy agreed, smiling. 'And I would love to hear you play for us. You know we have a grand piano in the Sculpture Gallery.'

'How do you feel living with a synthetic woman?' she asked Jack.

He chuckled and hugged her. 'Why don't we get married?' he said jokingly. 'We would be the first human-android couple.'

'I would like that, Jack, to be with you again. You are my love.' She kissed him.

'It won't be a legal ceremony,' Susan told them. 'There's a law against humans marrying androids.'

'I know, but it'll be a bit of fun and good for publicity if we can get this Project to work.' Jack chuckled.

'Hmm...' Nicolas faced him. 'If you are serious, you could have your wedding here in the Sculpture Gallery. And we have a vacant apartment in the West Wing, ideal while you're working here.'

'Sounds interesting. I guess this will make me a permanent part of your Lisbeth Project,' Jack said. 'To be with Helen, I will work and live at the Institute.'

Helen looked at Nicolas and Colin sternly. 'I have inside knowledge of how the quantum chip works. I'd happily work for the Institute if Jack is with me.' She paused. And I want to be a free person, not the property of the Institute.'

'I see,' Nicolas puffed. 'You are the heart of our research, my dear. And this Project has cost us millions.'

'I'm still your Lisbeth Project, here for your research, but I want to be a free person.'

'Very well. But I'll have a personal security team assigned to you. This I must insist on. We have to protect the Lisbeth Project from other interested parties. Do you agree?'

'I accept and understand your concern. I will live and work at the Institute with Jack. Thank you, Nicolas.'

Colin chuckled with a shake of his head. 'I guess you know more about that damn chip than any of us. Welcome aboard, Helen. And yes, I will be your best man at the wedding, no need to ask.'

———— ◆ ————

Jack moved most of his belongings into their apartment at the Institute, and Helen organised the place. They were left to settle in and make a home for a while. They decided there was no need to get married. Instead, Helen gave a private piano recital that proved a huge success. Only the research team knew she was a synthetic android. She passed easily as a human being.

He found her sitting at her bureau in the lounge using her laptop.

'What you doing?' he asked.

She looked around with a smile. 'I'm just discovering my past life as Vanessa. I still don't have those memories, but this information has restored some of the old me. Except I'm Helen, and I don't look like her. Does that matter to you?'

He shook his head and hugged her. 'It is your spirit, your soul that I love. However, you are beautiful, and you have amazing talents.'

She stood and kissed him. 'I cherish every moment with you, Jack. Your spirit, your soul, is entwined with my soul.'

'I feel that too.' He rubbed his forehead against her forehead. 'When you died, I didn't believe it. I felt you were still here. Even seeing your corpse in the morgue, I still felt you were out there, somewhere.' He frowned. 'I even went to a medium. There was a séance, and I thought you made contact, but the medium had a fit and passed out.'

She creased her brow and puckered. 'I think I kept trying to reach you. But the fire never stopped burning.'

'You are here now. This is your new life as the first conscious synthetic being.'

'It's not the same as being human. This form is dull and insensitive. Yet, I am getting used to living in this synthetic body.'

Jack's pager buzzed. Colin wanted them to visit the research labs.

———— ◆ ————

In the lab, Helen entered a cubicle to charge while Colin ran some diagnostic programs on her. Jack joined Susan and Rebecca by the bank of terminals.

'We've been working with the new Q-chips,' Susan told him excitedly. 'One is set up in this android's head matrix for the experiment.' She motioned to an open circuit board on the test bed with wires and interfaces linked to an active cubicle.

'How's it going?' he asked.

'The chip is functioning okay. We've tried a dozen times to get one of Rita's departed spirits to enter the chip, but it's not working as we hoped. Colin's running some diagnostics on Helen's chip to see if we've missed something.'

'Where is Rita?'

'Having lunch with Timothy. They'll be back later.'

'So, how are you interfacing the spirit with the chip?'

'We activate the chip in the Unit's matrix, then Rita and her inner guides work with a departed spirit to bond with the chip.'

'Any success?'

'One of her guides managed to cause the chip to fluctuate a little,' Rebecca said. 'But it couldn't bond or anchor with the chip.'

'We've scheduled a series of experiments using Rita over the next week or so. And we're still working with another Q-chip on the advanced Lisbeth project.'

'Good luck with that. I guess you don't need me for a while, and I need to sort out my London property. I've decided to sell the place. Which means transporting a grand piano and her artworks back here.'

'Is Helen going with you?'

'Yeah, with her personal minders. They come with us everywhere and can help clear out the place. Might take a few days or a week.'

Colin came over. 'That's done. Now I need to analyse the data.' He yawned, then looked at Jack. 'I hear you are off for a few days. Don't forget her portable charger.'

'One of her female minders takes care of that. I've got used to them being around. They're good company and look after her.'

'Have a good time.' He yawned again, then went back to his workstation.

Chapter Ten

A week later, Jack and Helen returned to the Institute. After settling in, they attended a group meeting in the library. Nicolas, Rita and the research team were sitting at the conference table. Nicolas rose and motioned them to sit.

Jack glanced at Rita, sensed the mood in the room, and guessed their research was not going well.

'So far, we've been unable to ensoul another Q-chip,' Nicolas said, then motioned to Rita, a chubby, ginger-haired woman in a green dress. She had dark eyes and wore rings on all her fingers and a large Ankh pendant around her neck.

'My spirit guides have been working on the transference,' she spoke with a slight northern accent. 'We have tried several willing souls for the experiment, but they can't anchor in the Q-chip. Their connection to the physical world has gone.'

'Yet Vanessa managed?' Jack said.

'My guides say Vanessa must have still been connected to the physical world. Maybe her love for you kept her here, earthbound. She didn't pass on.'

'Where does that leave us?' Timothy asked.

'We're still working with the chips on our advanced android research,' Colin reminded him.

'I think Rita might be right,' Helen said. 'I refused to move on and kept focused on my link with Jack and stayed in the fire.'

'There has to be a reason it worked for you,' Susan said, then looked at Rita. 'You say Vanessa died but didn't pass on?'

'My guides believe Vanessa was earthbound and managed to anchor her *silver cord* in the Q-chip before it dissipated.'

'What's this silver cord?' Colin asked.

'The etheric cord is how the soul anchors to a human foetus. When the body dies, the cord dissipates.'

'I don't understand spirituality,' Jack said. 'But this cord seems to be a link, like an interface that we all have while we are alive, and it dissipates when we die. So, my question is, would it be possible to transfer the cord from a living person into the Q-chip? Maybe someone near death would still have the cord attached and might be willing to experiment?'

After a tense silence, Rita cleared her throat and spoke softly, 'There are references in old occult scriptures concerning the transference of soul. It is believed that a few Hindu gurus practised this dark art of taking over someone's body.'

'How did they do that?' Colin asked, sounding sceptical. 'It's not possible.'

'Do your guides know?' Susan asked Rita.

'I'll ask.' She closed her eyes for several minutes before stiffening with a jolt. She opened her eyes wide and spoke in a gruff male voice. 'The old ones knew the forbidden art of transmigration. They used the door that opens both ways. We cannot pass on that knowledge.'

'Why not?' Colin asked.

'Because we don't know the key that unlocks that mystery. Jesus knew, and he, like the Buddha, had the power and unlocked the knowledge.' She chuckled, making a face. 'Your mind science has glossed over these deep mysteries. What you don't understand is ignored. Be warned, your path is leading to the dark side of the pit.' Rita choked and slumped on the table. When she sat up, she was shaking, her face was pale, and she seemed to be in a state of shock.

'You all right?' Susan asked her.

'I've got to go.' She stood and shook herself. 'I won't be coming back. My guides don't like what's going on here. Nor do I.' She left the room, leaving the doors open. Susan followed her out and shut the doors.

'Bloody mumbo jumbo,' Colin said. 'I knew this psychic stuff wouldn't work.'

'Wait!' Helen said and touched Jack's arm. 'I see...yes. There is a complex thread from the chip to this Unit. I feel it like a conduit. Could that be the cord Rita was talking about?'

'That could be it!' Jack looked at Nicolas. 'We have detected a thread from the Q-chip to the Unit. If we can detect that thread or cord in a human being.' He paused. 'We might be able to create a transference from a living human into the chip in a synthetic Unit.'

'If we could do that,' Timothy said almost excitedly. 'It would be an amazing discovery. We can't bring back the dead, but we could prolong the life of the living.'

'How do we go about this development?' Nicolas asked.

'We can set up a lab to investigate the possibility of this transference,' Colin said. 'We have registered the interface thread from the chip, but we need a human subject to experiment with to find this human cord. If it exists? Anyway, we'll also need some advanced brain scanning technology.'

'I'll volunteer,' Jack said.

'Why?' Nicolas asked with a look of surprise.

'The research will open my mind. And, if possible, I'd like to probe one of those Q-chips?' he said with mixed feelings of excitement and fear.

———◆———

Jack entered a modified cubicle in the lab, and the technicians wired him to the machine. Helen stood by the cubicle, looking concerned. Then Colin appeared with Susan.

'This cerebral scanning will be noisy, and there might be some pain. If it gets too much, press the red button or call out,' Susan told him.

'Why is this scan different?' he asked. They had used a variety of medical and research scans during the week. And this was, hopefully, their last scan.

'Courtesy of NASA. Nicolas pulled a few strings,' Colin said. 'It's experimental and registers some strange subspace energies and forces.'

'This even covers the etheric energy band.' Susan paused, looking concerned. 'However, they can't guarantee it is safe. There have been some casualties. Mostly, memory loss and confusion that lasted several hours or even a few days. But, out of thirty-seven volunteers, there was one fatality.'

'We're not sure if the scan caused his death because he may have had underlying health problems,' Colin said, then faced Jack. 'It's up to you. Do you want to go through with this or not?'

'Someone has to do this. And I want to probe a Q-chip after the scan. Can you have one connected to this cubicle? I want to see if there is a connection or whatever.'

'Okay, Jack. We got one installed. Tell me when you're ready, and I'll start the scan.'

'Jack.' Helen touched his face, then kissed him. 'I love you.'

For a moment, he felt a surge of dread, recalling when he first arrived and experienced a chilling fear of crossing a threshold into the unknown. He knew then it would come to something like this.

'You all right?' Susan asked.

'Yes, I'm fine,' he said, then smiled at Helen. 'You are my love, always.'

'Everything is ready,' Colin said.

'Let's do it.' Jack took a long, deep breath and closed his eyes. First, a low humming penetrated his skull and tingled along his spine for over ten minutes. Then pulses started flashing like tiny sparks in his mind. Suddenly, a kaleidoscope of fragmented colours burst into his consciousness and numbed his brain. While stunned, a fluctuation rippled through him, and a tremor of fear iced his heart. He felt a powerful jolt and slipped into a timeless ocean of intrinsic energy. Alone, he experienced his physical senses and body dissipating, and then his ability to think abruptly ceased. He had no mind, no feeling or sense of being. Just an acute knowingness remained that he was simply a point of awareness drifting into a silent, dark void.

'Jack, Jack, come back to me. Please,' a woman pleaded.

When his eyes opened, it took him a long time to focus because his vision was different. There was so much visual information that he found it difficult to identify objects and the people around him.

'Jack!' the woman snapped and shook him.

He inhaled deeply, closing his eyes, then sat up and realised he was still in the cubicle.

'Don't move. Just relax,' an older woman told him.

'What's happened to me?' he asked weakly.

'Thank God you've survived, Jack. It's me, Helen!'

He focused on her and felt a deep connection, but he didn't know who she was.

'Connect with your memory base,' a bearded man told him.

He focused within and found a pool of intelligent holographic memories. He gasped when he connected with that luminous pool, and his body shuddered with a chilling realisation. He was living in a synthetic android body. The shock made him groan and open his eyes.

'How did this happen?' he asked, feeling internally numb.

'We had no choice,' Colin said. 'We managed to identify the human cord, but your body died during that scan. We think that your illness in South America may have weakened your constitution. You had a violent seizure, and your heart stopped. When we couldn't revive you, we transferred your cord interface into this Q-chip.'

'Your cord anchored in the chip, and your neural net was pulled in,' Susan said with a troubled face. 'We don't understand what happened during the transference.'

Closing his eyes, he took a slow, deep breath and mentally called out his name as he exhaled. He experienced a rush of tingling energy momentarily, followed by incredible peace. Gradually, memories of his life as Jack Harper began to surface. From childhood to the present, he saw flashes of his life. Finally, he chuckled and opened his eyes.

'I have retained my memories and knowledge. I know who I am or was, but what am I now?'

'You are like me.' Helen took his hand and helped him out of the cubicle.

Looking around, he realised they were in his apartment at the Institute.

'How long has it been?' he asked, viewing his arms and moving his fingers.

'Seven days since your body died,' Susan replied. 'During that time, it took five days to finish growing this advanced synthetic form and two days to integrate the instinctual conditioning to control and function the Unit.' She touched his chest and said, 'Today, you were reborn, Jack.'

'The transference was a success,' Colin said, then narrowed his eyes and frowned. 'But we don't know how we did it. One of the Q-chips was connected to the cubicle for you to scan. When your body was dying, Helen connected with your cubicle and used her thread to help you bond with the Q-chip, and then it just happened. We didn't know if it had worked until we inserted the chip into this Unit.'

'I have no memory of the transference. I did experience dying. That was rather strange. Then I saw a soothing light and woke in this synthetic body.'

Nicolas and Timothy entered and came over.

'Jack is awake, and he has retained his memories. We did it!' Susan said excitedly.

'We didn't think it would work,' Timothy said, looking very pleased.

'How do you feel?' Nicolas asked Jack.

He looked at them and squinted. 'It's strange in this synthetic body, but I feel okay.'

'Good because we need to reproduce the experiment and understand the science involved,' Nicolas said. Then, he faced Jack. 'I want you in charge of the research team. You and Helen are the first human synthetics.'

Jack took a few tentative steps and stretched his back and arms. Then, looking around the living room, he realised that the Unit's instinctual programming was functioning, and he had complete control of the body.

'How does this feel compared to a human body?' Susan asked.

He closed his eyes for a few moments to get the internal feel of the synthetic form. Then he opened his eyes and chuckled. 'It's different, less sensitive, a bit strange at first, yet it has all the senses and the feel of being human. I breathe normally and can feel its two bio-mechanical hearts beating. I can get used to this synthetic form. And we can certainly enhance these bodies.'

'What about the Q-chip?' Colin asked.

Jack focused on the thread to the chip for a long time, and then he chuckled. 'There are some vague memories of an alien soul who used the chip for thousands of years. It is a jewel in the lotus where the soul can reside.'

Helen took his arm, and he smiled fondly at her.

'For a week, I thought I'd lost you,' she said, hugging him. 'Every day, I prayed for you to survive.'

'Well, I'm still here.' He kissed her. 'And we are the new synthetic humanity.' He looked at Nicolas and Timothy. 'This is the beginning of the New Age. Can you, guys, imagine what the future will be like? Through these Q-chips, these jewels in the lotus, we have discovered immortality!'

END

ABOUT THE AUTHOR

During my youth, I lived in a haunted Victorian house that inspired my fascination with the supernatural. In my early years, I studied various world religions, spiritual paths, and belief systems in an attempt to uncover the meaning of life. Eventually, after growing weary and abandoning my long search, a profound realisation occurred that transformed my understanding of everything.

Years later, after experiencing numerous bizarre paranormal events and gaining some interesting insights, I began writing fantasy stories that incorporate elements of the occult and spirituality. I aim to entertain and inspire others to explore the strange nature of our extraordinary existence.

Life on Earth is a beautiful learning adventure and a playground for the soul, yet it differs significantly from cosmic reality. Those who recall our origins beyond this planet can appreciate how enchanting and occasionally bittersweet physical life can be.

David (dbm)

Also, by this author:

GRIMOIRE *The Haunting of Rickland Manor.*

Gavin purchased the Victorian property as a promising investment and moved in with his American girlfriend, Cynthia. When their friends Sally and Raul came to stay for a few days, Gavin took them on a tour of the house. In the dimly lit cellar, they discovered a bricked-up door behind one of the wine racks. Intrigued, they spent several hours working to open it.

Inside, Gavin switched on the lights, revealing a spacious, empty room illuminated by fluorescent lighting. Two large, red outer circles, surrounding a black pentagon, were inlaid in the marble floor. The dusty, stale air thickened around them as they entered the room. Cautiously, they were drawn toward a dark, arched alcove that emitted a faint, humming magnetic energy, which intensified as they approached.

Unknowingly, their presence had triggered the awakening of an ancient grimoire rite that had remained dormant for years. As they left that secret, eerie room, they were unaware that they had become ensnared in an occult web where the physical and supernatural realms were dangerously entwined.

SHARED RECALL *The Law of the ONE.*

When two strangers meet by chance, they begin to recall a life they shared before the biblical flood. Byron, a single parent with two children, and Silvie, a gay schoolteacher in a relationship with Grace, embark on a journey to explore these vivid shared memories. Their past as lovers during that extraordinary life complicates their current relationships. Suddenly, an ancient adversary they encountered during that turbulent period reemerges with deadly intent, dramatically altering their lives forever

NIGHT SIDE OF EDEN

Edward, once a prominent celebrity in the world of psychic phenomena, is reluctantly drawn back from his reclusive life to find a young woman who has been kidnapped. Her captor, Mark Skully, is a sorcerer deeply skilled in black magic, and he embarks on a vengeful occult war against Edward and his loved ones. As the stakes escalate, Edward faces a devastating choice: to save his daughter from the perilous realm of the dragon djinn, he must sacrifice his human soul.

May you all, in your own way, discover the spirit of freedom.

For those interested, you can visit my website: https://artdaja.com/index.html

Printed in Dunstable, United Kingdom